...shook his head. "Better not chance it. Truth is, between the Trivial Pursuit and the cards, I'm tired of playing games."

She stared at him for a moment, then gave him a smile so downright appealing, it warmed some cold, dark spot deep inside him. She reached across the table and took his hand, wrapping her fingers around his palm to give him a gentle squeeze.

He drew a sharp breath. Her touch was like fire; it turned his blood to liquefied heat and set his nerve endings deliciously aflame. Then his heart started to pound as if he'd just received an intravenous injection of pure adrenaline.

"So am I," she said huskily. "Terribly tired of playing this silly little game of ours."

She leaned in a little closer. "So tell me, darling," she murmured. "Just what do you suggest we do about it?"

SUPER ROMANCE

WHAT ARE *LOVESWEPT* ROMANCES?

*They are stories of true romance and touching emotion. We
believe those two very important ingredients are constants in
our highly sensual and very believable stories in the LOVE-
SWEPT line. Our goal is to give you, the reader, stories of
consistently high quality that may sometimes make you laugh,
sometimes make you cry, but are always fresh and creative and
contain many delightful surprises within their pages.*

*Most romance fans read an enormous number of books. Those
they truly love, they keep. Others may be traded with friends
and soon forgotten. We hope that each LOVESWEPT romance will be a treasure—a "keeper." We will always try to
publish*

LOVE STORIES YOU'LL NEVER FORGET
BY AUTHORS YOU'LL ALWAYS REMEMBER

The Editors

WILD
AT
HEART

FAYE HUGHES

BANTAM BOOKS
NEW YORK · TORONTO · LONDON · SYDNEY · AUCKLAND

WILD AT HEART
A Bantam Book / February 1996

LOVESWEPT *and the wave design are registered trademarks of*
Bantam Books, a division of Bantam Doubleday Dell Publishing Group,
Inc. Registered in U.S. Patent and Trademark Office and elsewhere.

ISBN 0-553-44527-8

Published simultaneously in the United States and Canada

Bantam Books *are published by Bantam Books, a division of Bantam Dou-*
bleday Dell Publishing Group, Inc. Its trademark, consisting of the words
"Bantam Books" and the portrayal of a rooster, is Registered in U.S.
Patent and Trademark Office and in other countries. Marca Registrada.
Bantam Books, 1540 Broadway, New York, New York 10036.

PRINTED IN THE UNITED STATES OF AMERICA

OPM   0 9 8 7 6 5 4 3 2 1

AUTHOR'S NOTE

Dear Readers:

Clark Gable. Claudette Colbert. A jaded reporter in the midst of a career skid unexpectedly stumbles across the biggest story of the year—and the grandest love of any lifetime—when his path crosses that of a spoiled debutante on the run. *It Happened One Night* has always been one of my favorite movies, so when the editors at Bantam asked me to write a book inspired by my favorite Treasured Tale, the choice was easy.

As you read WILD AT HEART, you'll notice that I've taken many liberties in telling my version of the romance at the heart of *It Happened One Night*. Maggie Thorpe, tabloid darling and undisputed "deb of the decade", is not eloping to meet a thoroughly inappropriate fiance. Nor is Jake Wilder, an investigative journalist currently stuck working for a tabloid, eloping with her so he can get an exclusive for his paper. To the contrary. Both Maggie and Jake are on the run because Jake has uncovered a political scandal that threatens them both and must remain out of sight until the big story breaks.

Although the storyline is radically different, I've tried to keep the spirit of Peter and Ellen alive in my Jake and Maggie, mostly because my focus is more on sophisticated humor and sparkling repartee rather than on nail-biting suspense. You'll see what I mean when Jake strings an old blanket between the lumpy bed and lumpier still easy chair to create a bound-to-crumble wall of Jericho in their one room mountain cabin, just as Peter once did. (In fact in the ultimate homage to their spirit and the movie that has inspired me for so long, I've even had Jake and Maggie select Peter and Ellen Warren as their aliases!)

Many of you have written to tell me how much you enjoy the romantic adventures I write for Loveswept. I hope WILD AT HEART will please you as much as my other books have.

All the best,

Faye Hughes

Faye Hughes

ONE

There were two things Jake Wilder knew he had to remember when trying to crash an invitation-only political fund-raiser. The first was that the bouncers often carried nasty little service revolvers in the waistbands of their tuxedos. The second was that if he made it past the front door without getting busted, he probably didn't have to worry about the bouncers.

At least that was what Jake hoped would be the case. Truth was, he'd never had much chance to test his theory.

Until now.

Muttering a quick prayer under his breath, Jake ducked behind a heavyset, silver-haired matron in a blue beaded gown who was waiting to show her invitation to the nice people manning the entrance to the Universal Hilton's grand ballroom. Moving in step with her as she made her way along the

slow-moving receiving line—and careful to keep
well out of view of the burly-looking security
guard—Jake bided his time.

He figured he needed only a second or two, just
long enough for the guard's attention to be diverted elsewhere.

Jake glanced over his shoulder to see if any
other invitees to the gala September fund-raiser
were straggling in, but the long hallway behind him
was still empty. When Jake glanced back, the guard
had turned away to ask a member of the senator's
staff a question.

Taking a deep breath, Jake rushed forward and
slipped through the open double doors and into the
ballroom. Then he waited, afraid even to breathe.

Ten seconds passed.

Twenty.

When no one seemed the wiser to his arrival,
Jake exhaled his pent-up breath and tried to relax.
Piece of cake, he told himself, dusting off the lapels
of his dinner jacket. Then, unable to resist a self-
congratulatory grin, Jake started to weave his way
through the milling bands of well-dressed merry-
makers.

From the looks of things, the thousand-dollar-
a-plate fund-raiser to benefit the reelection campaign of Senator Todd McNichols was just getting
started. There were nearly three hundred people
scheduled to attend, not counting the members of
the press, who were forced to wait in a holding area
adjacent to the ballroom.

Jake, however, hadn't been invited to do even that. It seemed the senator's staff didn't want any representatives of the *Los Angeles Sentinel*—or any other *tabloid*, they'd added with an upper-crust sneer—to be anywhere near their private little party.

Unfortunately for the senator's campaign staff, the lack of an engraved invitation had never been enough to stop Jake from getting a story.

Nodding a greeting to a middle-aged couple deep in conversation as he squeezed past them, Jake made his way to the center of the room. Then he glanced around the ballroom, which was decorated to its rafters with red, white, and blue balloons. Full-color posters of the thirty-eight-year-old bachelor senator's smiling face were plastered everywhere, along with McNichols's trademark campaign promise: *One honest man can make a difference.*

Yeah, right, Jake thought, grabbing a glass of Chablis from the tray of a passing waiter.

Nice slogan, only there wasn't anything *honest* about the good senator or his campaign. If Jake had his way, the whole state would soon know about it too.

He took a sip of wine and scanned the crowded room again, just in time to see the burly-looking guard from the main entrance moving swiftly toward him with a determined look on his face.

Damn.

Jake looked around, hoping to find an escape hatch. No such luck.

"Excuse me, sir," came the ever-so-polite voice of the guard a few seconds later. "I don't believe your invitation has been checked."

Jake smiled, lowering his glass of wine. "My invitation?"

"Yes, sir. I don't believe it has been checked against the guest list. May I see it, please?"

The man was the epitome of graciousness, but Jake knew it was just for show. The guard knew that Jake had crashed the party. He probably knew that Jake was a reporter non gratis too. Unless Jake produced an invitation or came up with some plausible explanation for why he didn't have one, he would likely find himself trying to explain it all to the LAPD before the night was over.

Jake turned up his smile a few degrees and laid on the southern charm his mama had always claimed he was blessed with.

"Well, I—" Jake handed the guard his glass of Chablis and proceeded to check the inside of his dinner jacket. "Why, I believe my date must have it."

Jake glanced over the guard's shoulder at his nonexistent date and started to wave.

"Oh, darlin'. Come on over here for a moment and show this nice man our invitation."

The guard turned just as Jake knew he would, giving Jake a chance to make his getaway.

Not wasting the opportunity, Jake quickly maneuvered through the crowd and out the service entrance into the back hallway. The clanging of pots and pans rang out from the kitchen several yards away, along with the hum of voices. Jake found an unmarked door, tried the handle, and slipped into the small linen closet just as the double doors leading to the ballroom swung closed behind him.

Jake reached for the light switch on the wall and flipped it on, then sank onto a metal cart filled with folded tablecloths and sighed. He supposed he might as well get comfortable.

He had a funny feeling that he was going to be there for a long while.

He was, by far, the handsomest party crasher she'd ever seen.

Unable to resist a grin, Maggie Thorpe lowered her wine goblet and stared after the tall, muscular, black-haired man who'd just bolted out the service entrance of the grand ballroom. She watched him dart into a storage room of some kind and close the door, leaving the guard who'd been talking with him seconds before scratching the close-cropped hairs on his head in apparent confusion.

Maggie laughed.

She had little doubt that the guy the guard was looking for was a party crasher, just as she had little doubt that the party crasher was a reporter. He was probably working for some tabloid too, Maggie deduced, rising to her feet.

After being dubbed the "Debutante of the De-

cade" by one of the rag sheets some ten years before—and then being relentlessly hounded by
swarms of tabloid reporters for virtually every day
of her life thereafter—she'd learned to recognize
the breed much the way a botanist learns to recognize the different types of flora in his garden.

She'd also learned that the easiest way to handle
reporters—better make that the *only* way to handle
reporters—was to simply cooperate with their requests for comments and photographs and hope
that, like a dreaded trip to the dentist, it would all
be over fairly quickly. Because nothing, not threats
of legal action, not temper tantrums—not even at-
tempts to outrun them in a jazzy little sports car—
was likely ever to deter a reporter once he was committed to getting a story.

Maggie grinned.

Although if any of the tabloid reporters who'd
ever chased after her had looked like this one, with
his broad shoulders and bluer-than-blue eyes, she
might not have put up such a struggle.

Not, she was quick to reassure herself as she
grabbed the bottle of wine and an empty glass from
her table and started toward the service entrance,
that any amount of masculine charm and just-to-
die-for good looks would change what she had to
do right now—namely to ask him to leave the party
before a mini scandal erupted and cast a pall over
Todd's big evening.

Ordinarily, Maggie couldn't have cared less
who crashed the fund-raiser. To tell the truth, she'd

have probably ordered a bowl of popcorn and settled back to root for the tabloid reporter, just for the entertainment value alone. But she'd promised her father that she'd see to it Todd's fund-raisers went off without a hitch while her parents were on an anniversary cruise down the Amazon, and that was precisely what she intended to do.

After all, the romantic getaway was the first her parents had taken in almost fourteen years. For as far back as Maggie could remember, her workaholic father had either postponed family vacations or simply bailed on both her and her mom at the last minute, citing the demands of running Thorpe Industries or a new crisis in whichever political campaign he was supporting at the time. Even though Maggie had never doubted her father's love, she had resented his too-frequent absences and had vowed a long time ago never to become involved with a man whose career was more important to him than she was.

For years, both she and her mother had tried to convince her father to slow down his hectic pace without much success. Luckily, a bad case of indigestion masking itself as a heart attack six months earlier had accomplished what their nagging couldn't, and he had rearranged his priorities. When he had asked Maggie to pinch hit for him while he took her mother off on a second honeymoon, Maggie had been only too happy to oblige— even if political speeches and fund-raisers did bore her silly.

Family was family.

And the contribution she'd managed to wrangle from Thorpe Industries for Pet Haven would keep the animal rescue fund she'd co-founded back in Marin County in kibble for an entire year.

Taking a sip of wine, Maggie glanced over her shoulder to make certain the guard wasn't following her. He wasn't. She pushed open the swinging double doors to the service entrance and walked down the hallway, her high heels clicking out a sharp staccato rhythm against the linoleum. She stopped when she came to the closed door she'd seen the reporter go through a few minutes earlier.

She tucked the wine bottle and extra goblet under her arm and rapped once against the wood paneling of the door.

"May I come in?"

A muffled curse followed.

Her grin grew wider. "I'll take that as a yes," she murmured under her breath.

She opened the door and slipped inside the small linen closet before she could change her mind, pulling the door firmly closed behind her.

"Hello," she said brightly.

The first thing she noticed about him was his size. He was big. Much bigger, in fact, than he'd appeared to be back in the ballroom—and much more imposing a figure too. He was a good head taller than her, probably somewhere around six foot two, she thought, letting her gaze slide over him . . . and over all those inches of solid muscular flesh and undeniable masculine virility. Too bad he was a reporter, she told herself.

He looked to be in his early thirties, probably only a few years older than her own twenty-seven. And he was even more handsome than she'd originally thought, although she now realized that he was much more than some pretty-boy matinee-idol type. He was the kind of man who emanated masculinity and inner strength the way a light bulb did luminescence.

The kind of man who, once met, she imagined would be damn hard to forget.

His face was lean and angular except for the Cary Grant–like cleft in his chin. He wore his longish, thick black hair parted on the side and slicked back from his forehead, which only seemed to emphasize the startling intensity of his blue eyes.

Arctic blue eyes, she decided, since they seemed frosted over just now with enough ice to freeze fire.

Maggie gave him a smile. "I hate to be the bearer of bad news, but you're never going to get away with it."

He scowled at her. "Get away with what?"

His voice was an appealing if chilly baritone, and the accent unmistakably southern, although she couldn't place its state of origin just then.

"Why, crashing the fund-raiser," she said matter-of-factly.

Maggie set her wineglass on top of a metal storage shelf and handed him the empty goblet.

"That is what you're trying to do, isn't it? Because I couldn't help but notice your little encounter with the guard outside."

A few seconds passed, then the suggestion of a smile slowly began to replace his scowl.

"What encounter?" he asked. "The guard was merely helping me locate my table."

"Uh-huh," she said, still trying to keep her tone light and teasing. "So why'd you make a beeline for the linen closet the moment the guard's back was turned? Or are you actually planning to suggest that *this* is where the seating committee placed you?"

"Well, I . . ."

"I know they said they were running short on tables tonight, but this is more than a little absurd, don't you think?"

The ice in his Arctic-tinged eyes began to melt, revealing the most beguiling pair of baby blues she'd ever seen. Then his smile started to deepen.

"I guess it is at that," he said.

She poured him a glass of Chablis and topped off her own goblet.

"Look, don't get me wrong," she said. "I thought you were great. Better even than Woodward and Bernstein in their prime. But we need to face facts here, unpleasant though they may be. You're never going to be able to get back into the ballroom without being spotted by the guard. And since there's damn little point in your spending the remainder of the evening cooped up in a linen closet, I suggest we have a glass of wine, chat a bit, and then you leave through the back entrance before anyone catches on."

He stared at her for a moment longer, then he started to laugh.

The sound was so low and undeniably appealing that it made what seemed like a whole flock of butterflies start to take flight in her stomach.

"Well, at least the bouncers at this place are getting better looking," he drawled, taking a sip of wine. "That's something to be grateful for, I suppose."

His voice had softened and taken on a husky-tinged quality that she found hard to resist. It reminded her of some fine old brandy that her father kept under lock and key in his liquor cabinet.

All smooth and rich with enough kick to it to send shivers up and down her spine.

"I'll take that as a compliment," she said, feeling herself begin to flush.

She set her glass on the metal cabinet and extended her hand.

"Allow me to introduce myself. I'm Maggie—"

"Thorpe," he supplied with a smile so downright charming, it nearly took her breath away. "Yeah, I know. Although it took me a while to recognize you without all the paparazzi hanging around you."

She laughed. "I had to give them the night off. Union rules."

His fingers wrapped around her open palm and gently squeezed, sending a tingling warmth radiating up her arm and straight through to her very core.

She caught a whiff of his cologne just then. It was a crisp, clean, and utterly masculine scent that seemed to intensify the dizzying effects of the simple handshake a hundredfold.

Their gazes met, held for a moment. Then he slowly released her hand.

"And you are . . . ?" she prompted, feeling her flush begin to deepen.

"Wilder," he said, sounding as though his equilibrium had taken as much of a direct hit as hers had suddenly done. "Jake Wilder. Of the *Los Angeles Sentinel.*"

His name was vaguely familiar, although she couldn't quite place it right then.

"It's a pleasure to meet you, Jake Wilder," she said softly.

She sat down on a linen cart—it was the closest thing the closet had to a chair—and motioned for Jake to do the same on the one directly opposite her.

He regarded her cautiously for a moment, then slowly complied.

"You know, it's funny," she said. "I thought I knew all the reporters for the *Sentinel.* Don't Bob Liebowitz and Sandy Brenner cover the entertainment news?"

At least they'd been the ones who'd hounded her all summer long two years before. They, like every other tabloid reporter in the country, had been trying to get proof of a nonexistent romance between her and Charlie Darnell, an action superstar whom she'd met at a Beverly Hills fund-raiser for Actors and Others for Animals.

Maggie had been planning to open Pet Haven back in the Bay area. Charlie, as a major—though always anonymous—contributor to similar concerns in Los Angeles County, had been something of a godsend to her in terms of putting her in contact with all the right people to make Pet Haven become a reality.

"Yeah, they do," Jake said. "Cover the entertainment news for the *Sentinel*, I mean."

He took a sip of wine and eyed her over the rim of his glass for a few seconds. It was a wary look, the kind you'd give a large, unfamiliar dog who'd just wandered over to you. You wanted to reach out and pet him, but you weren't all that sure if he would try to bite your hand or give it a friendly lick once you made the attempt.

"I'm an investigative journalist," he added.

"And they sent you *here*?"

He started to bristle.

"Relax, Jake," she said, motioning him back down. "It's not a crack against the *Sentinel*. It's just that there's *nothing* worth investigating at these things, except maybe why a stringy chicken dinner and a couple of glasses of domestic Chablis cost over a thousand bucks a person. Why, I've been to three of the senator's last fund-raisers—including one over Labor Day weekend—and the only thing remotely newsworthy happened back in San Francisco last Wednesday night."

She leaned forward. Their knees lightly brushed together. She could feel the heat of his body seeping through the black bugle-beaded fabric of her evening gown and tried to resist a shiver.

"A city alderman bumped into one of the waiters," she said in a low whisper as though she were revealing state secrets. "The poor guy lost his balance and nearly dropped his toupee into somebody's bowl of soup."

"I, ah, see your point."

Jake's gaze locked with hers. She was amazed then that she'd ever thought his eyes were frigid and cold. Because now they seemed to her to be as warm and inviting as an azure sea.

She felt those butterflies in her stomach take flight again. Her heart started to pound.

"A nearly dislodged toupee's hardly front-page material," he said, giving her another smile.

It was a nice smile too, Maggie decided. Friendly. Engaging—and sexy as hell.

"So tell me something, Maggie darlin'," he said, his southern drawl becoming even more pronounced.

Mississippi, she thought. No, Georgia. And so wickedly seductive, she now knew why Gladys Knight used to sing about taking that midnight train back home.

He leaned toward her. "Why do you keep attending the good senator's fund-raisers if they're as boring as you claim they are?"

"Oh," she said. "Let's just say I'm doing a favor for my father."

A favor that seemed to be getting larger by the second—although she wasn't minding it quite as much now as she had about ten minutes earlier.

"And what about you?" she asked. "Why were you trying to crash the fund-raiser?"

Jake shrugged. "Oh, that."

He settled back on his cart and raised his glass of wine to stare down into its golden contents.

"Yes, that."

She took a long swallow of wine. The tantalizing scent of his aftershave floated around her, fogging her senses, making her feel almost giddy.

"Just what kind of dirt are you hoping to dig up on poor old Todd anyway?" she teased.

Not that she imagined Jake would find any. She knew Todd. In a moment of supreme weakness she'd agreed to go out on a couple of dates with him—much to her father's approval and her mother's utter amazement—so Maggie knew first-hand just how unbelievably boring Senator Todd McNichols really was.

A few seconds passed.

Then Jake downed his wine.

"Oh, nothing much," he said calmly, setting the empty goblet on the floor. "Just the kind of dirt that will bury both his hopes for reelection and his entire political career with one shovelful."

Maggie blinked, feeling as though she'd just been doused with a bucket of ice water.

She settled back on her cart. "I, ah, don't suppose you'd care to elaborate?"

The closet door swung open and banged against the wall, chipping off several inches of white paint. Maggie jumped, muttered a curse, and nearly spilled the glass of wine all over her dress.

She turned in time to see the burly security guard who'd been tracking Jake earlier that evening barrel his way into the closet.

Raymond Kingfisher, the senator's reptilian campaign manager, was fast behind him.

"Okay, buddy," the guard said with a growl, placing his hands on his hips. "No more Mr. Nice Guy. I want you out of the hotel. Now."

Jake's hands began to tighten into fists. He started to rise.

"Last time I checked," he growled right back, "the hotel was open to the general public."

Great, Maggie thought, glancing from one man to the other. Just great. This was really all she needed. She had a tabloid reporter out looking for the senator's blood, and a guard about to open a vein, while the man who was supposed to be responsible for preventing such PR disasters just stood there and watched.

She could even see the morning headlines of the *Sentinel* now. *Brawl at McNichols Fund-raiser: Security Pummels Reporter out to Expose Senator.*

Worse than that, Maggie could also hear the

stream of epithets that would fall from her father's lips once he heard about the incident . . . and his voice would likely hit a new octave or two when he found out about her role in the debacle.

Maggie glanced from Jake to the guard again, then deposited her wineglass on the floor and jumped to her feet, positioning herself squarely between the two men.

She placed her hands on her hips and glared at the guard. "How dare you intrude on a private conversation!"

The guard looked sheepish for a moment. "Sorry, Miss Thorpe," he said. "But he's a gate-crasher who tried to sneak past me earlier."

"He did no such thing," Maggie lied.

And quite believably too, she thought.

Raymond Kingfisher positively glowered. "The man is a reporter, *Ms.* Thorpe. And he works for the *Sentinel*, for Pete's sake! I can't begin to imagine what you think you're doing sharing wine in a linen closet with him, but—"

"I know precisely who and what he is, Raymond," Maggie interrupted coolly.

She'd never much cared for Raymond Kingfisher, didn't much care for the supercilious way he had of dealing with his subordinates or for the way he was looking at her and Jake just now.

"His name is Jake Wilder," Maggie said. "And he happens to be my escort for this evening. And as for what we were doing in the linen closet, well, no, I don't think you *could* begin to imagine it."

Maggie reached for Jake's arm and gave him a tug. He resisted at first, then came with her.

No doubt about it, she decided as they cruised past a stunned-looking Raymond and the suddenly silent security guard, her father owed her big-time.

In fact, the amount of his contribution to Pet Haven had just tripled in size.

TWO

Things weren't turning out the way he'd planned.

His body still tense, his adrenaline pumping—but with Maggie's warm fingertips still pressing firmly into his arm—Jake slowly followed her out of the linen closet and into the back hallway. He glanced over his shoulder at Kingfisher and the guard as they turned toward the rear entrance of the ballroom.

The guard seemed unaffected by the turn of events, but the campaign manager didn't look the least bit happy. In fact, Kingfisher looked annoyed as hell that Jake was being allowed into McNichols's private fund-raiser—and as an invited guest of the daughter of one of the senator's most influential backers too. Jake knew there wasn't much Kingfisher could do to change the situation.

Later, however, once Maggie's attentions were diverted elsewhere, Jake figured that he might find himself out in the alley, staring down the wrong end of the security guard's revolver.

Kingfisher's scowl deepened. "The senator isn't going to like this, *Ms.* Thorpe," he called out.

The implied threat in his voice came through loud and clear.

Maggie just shrugged it off. "And my father will like your impertinence at questioning my choice in escorts even less, Raymond, I assure you."

She gave the door to the service entrance a sharp push with the palm of her free hand.

"Now, come along, *Jake darling*," she added in a saccharine-sweet drawl. "I'm afraid we've dawdled back here long enough as it is."

She steered Jake into the grand ballroom before Kingfisher could say another word.

Jake couldn't help but grin as the door swung closed behind them with a soft *whoosh* of air. He had to admit that for a pampered little debutante used to having the world at her feet, Maggie Thorpe wasn't half bad for having around in a crunch.

For that matter, with her impish sense of humor and healthy disrespect for authority, she could become a woman after his own heart.

Jake glanced down at her, and his grin grew wider. She was probably the best-looking thing on any two continents.

He sighed. Too bad she wasn't his type. He'd developed a severe allergic reaction to pampered little debutantes several years earlier . . . and

Margaret Lynn Thorpe, with her well-publicized history for leaving a string of broken hearts and elevated body temperatures almost everywhere she went, had the reputation for being the biggest little deb of them all.

What's more, she was a darling of the tabloids, a bona fide media sensation. The press loved her because she was rich and beautiful and delightfully outrageous, and having her picture on the cover sold a lot of copies. Maggie had moved from San Francisco's society pages to national prominence ten years before, when she was seventeen. *Vanity Fair* had run a story on her and a stunt that she and a group of other little debs had pulled in Frisco, something about pink bubble bath in a public fountain and a moonlit swim. The public had eaten it up and asked for more. The tabloids—and Maggie—had been only too happy to comply.

She had reached her PR pinnacle two years previously when she'd had her fling with Charlie Darnell. Her face had been plastered across the front page of every tabloid in the country, including the *Sentinel*, for virtually the entire summer. Lately, however, she'd been keeping a low profile, much to the dismay of the *Sentinel*'s sales staff.

"We're seated up front," she said, weaving her way around a chair blocking their path without missing a beat. "Near the senator's table."

Jake grinned. "Naturally."

Where else would one seat the deb of the decade, except near the center of attention?

Jake let his gaze slide along her honey-blond hair, which cascaded past her shoulders in silken waves.

Of course, once everyone in the room got a good look at her, he had no doubt that Maggie would likely become the center of attention regardless of where she sat.

She really was a beautiful woman, Jake thought with unabashed male appreciation. Tall and elegant but completely approachable, not distant or aloof. Her hair looked soft to the touch. Thick. Lustrous as gold. The kind of hair a man liked to weave his fingers through when he kissed a woman long and hard.

Not that he was actually thinking about kissing her, Jake was quick to reassure himself. It was just that her lips looked perfect for kissing. They were full and generous and, at the moment, they were curved in a naughty smile that he found very appealing.

He let his gaze drop farther along her body, lingering at the gentle swell of her breasts and the provocative curve of her hips. It would take little imagination on a man's part to picture his hands sliding slowly around her hips to hold her close to him, or to feel her soft breasts pressing intimately against his bare chest.

His grin deepened. Now that he had time to think about it, he decided that all of her looked pretty damned appealing. Her skin was smooth and lightly tanned, and her hazel eyes sparkled with the promise of more delightfully sinful mayhem to come.

It was a promise echoed by her choice in evening attire: her black bugle-beaded gown hugged her body in such an openly sensuous way, it could make a saint start thinking about sinning.

Jake felt his body begin to grow tighter, harder than it had in a long time. He took a slow, deep breath.

This is crazy, he told himself. *Absolutely nuts.* The woman was a spoiled little debutante, another Alyssa, for crying out loud, and he was letting his hormones cloud his common sense like some high school kid hot to lose his virginity.

"Relax, Jake," Maggie whispered as though she were reading his thoughts. "This won't be as bad as you think. Trust me."

He quickly exhaled. "What?" he asked hoarsely.

They had reached their table, which was just to the right of the dais and the senator's campaign party. The waiters were in the process of serving the salads, so most of the seats were already taken except for the two at the end of the table. Several guests flicked their gazes in Jake and Maggie's direction then smiled in recognition of Maggie, and went back to their food and their own conversations.

"Raymond," Maggie said, tossing her head in the direction of the dais. "He wouldn't dare cause a scene now."

Jake glanced over in time to see Kingfisher take his seat next to a smiling Senator McNichols, who was deep in conversation with the mayor of Los Angeles.

"Just enjoy the food . . . or try to anyway," she suggested, releasing his arm.

She gave him a smile that lit up her whole face; the lights in her hazel eyes started to twinkle and dance. He found himself relaxing.

"Chances are pretty good that we're getting chicken," she went on. "Oh, they'll probably call it something very continental-sounding," she said with a toss of her hand, "but it'll still be the same stringy chicken they always serve at these things."

Her voice held those soft, feminine cadences she'd used on him in the linen closet before Kingfisher's arrival. Funny, but it didn't matter so much what she said, Jake realized with a smile. He found the sound of her voice playfully seductive; it stroked his masculine ego like nothing else ever had before, sending his already overactive imagination racing even further out of control.

Her shoulder brushed against his chest as she sat down, sending fiery shivers spiraling around him and leaving a trace of her perfume to linger afterward. Roses, he thought, taking a deep breath of its intoxicating scent. Dozens of them, but not so strong as to be overwhelming.

It was a fragrance as expensively erotic as she was herself, the kind that needed only one good whiff to insinuate itself directly into a man's soul, where it could wreak untold amounts of havoc with his emotional defenses.

The kind of scent that could easily lead a man to become just another notch on some little deb's gold-plated lipstick case if he didn't watch his step.

Jake scowled and shook his head, trying to clear his mind from thoughts of Maggie.

It didn't seem to work though.

"Why are you doing this?" he asked, slipping onto the brocade-covered seat beside her. "Sticking your neck out for me, I mean."

She gave him a grin. "Maybe I have a fondness for tabloid reporters." She lifted her water glass and slowly took a sip.

He regarded her for a moment. Then he smiled.

"And maybe you're just hoping to get your name back in the papers," he countered, keeping his voice as low and playful as hers had been. "It's been, what? A couple of years now since you were front-page news? Maybe you're planning another one of your infamous Maggie Thorpe exploits to get back on the front page of the *Sentinel*."

She laughed.

The sound was rich and full, and it tripped up and down his spine like a lover's caress. He decided that he liked hearing her laugh.

He decided that he liked a lot of things about her.

"I've never clamored for a headline in my entire life," she said. "And if I wanted a story done about

me in the *Sentinel*, all I'd have to do is call Bob
Liebowitz or Sandy Brenner. They'll turn cartwheels in their enthusiasm to get over here."

Maggie had him there. Liebowitz and Brenner
would have kept their wives waiting at the altar on
their respective wedding days if they thought they
could get an interview with Maggie Thorpe. And
the *Sentinel*'s sales staff would have probably turned
a few cartwheels themselves over the prospect of
the added revenue the story would bring.

Jake frowned. "So why—?"

One of the waiters set a green salad in front of
Jake, then slid another in front of Maggie, halting
Jake in mid-query.

Maggie just shrugged. "Buy me a drink after the
fund-raiser," she said, her hazel eyes twinkling like
mad. "We'll talk about it."

Then she lifted her fork and speared a lettuce
leaf.

Before Jake could press her for anything further, a gray-haired man leaned across the table.

"A pleasure to see you, as always, Maggie," he
said, "even if it is something of a surprise. I didn't
think political fund-raisers were your particular cup
of tea."

"They're not." Maggie smiled. "Hello, David.
Lucille," she said, nodding to the well-made-up
red-haired woman seated next to him. "I still think
attending these fund-raisers is more boring than
watching cheese age." She cast a sidelong glance at

Jake. "However, thanks to Jake here, this one is proving to be a lot more exciting than most."

The other couple directed politely curious smiles in Jake's direction. He just smiled back.

"Actually," Maggie went on, "I'm pinch-hitting for Father tonight. He's taken Mother off on a second honeymoon, otherwise he wouldn't have missed this for the world—you know how he dotes on Todd."

"A second honeymoon! How lovely," Lucille murmured. "Did Mitsy make him take her someplace terribly romantic, I hope?"

"They're on a cruise down the Amazon," Maggie said. "Absolutely incommunicado for the next two weeks. Last time I spoke with them, they said they were having the time of their lives."

Maggie then made the introductions. Jake had seen David Mayron's name in the financial section of the *Times* regularly enough to know that the man was worth millions . . . and that he liked to spend a lot of those millions financing political campaigns such as McNichols's bid for reelection.

"Jake Wilder . . ." David said thoughtfully, racking his brain for a memory. "You know, your name sounds awfully familiar."

Jake started to tense. He didn't like the direction in which their conversation was headed.

"Maybe I've just got that kind of name," he said. Then he took another sip of water and slid the glass back onto the table.

"Or maybe you've read some of his work,"

Maggie suggested, stabbing another lettuce leaf. "Jake's an investigative reporter for the *Los Angeles Sentinel*."

"For the *Sentinel*?" Lucille gave an embarrassed laugh. "Well, how . . . nice. I'm afraid we don't subscribe to that one though."

"That's okay, I don't subscribe myself," Jake said wryly. "But a lot of other people apparently do. The last I heard, our circulation rivaled that of the *Times*."

"Oh, I'm sure it appeals to a certain element," David said.

Maggie arched her eyebrows. "*A certain element?*" she repeated, reaching for the bread basket. She removed a dinner roll and placed it on her plate, then passed the basket to Jake.

"Really, David," she said. "You're talking about the people who keep Jake here employed. Now, I personally like the *Sentinel* . . . even if it has been, as someone recently pointed out to me, over two years since they've run a cover story on me."

Jake laughed, then took a roll and set the basket back on the table.

"Oh, no offense intended," David said quickly. "While its format doesn't appeal to me now, the *Sentinel* used to be a fine paper. It could be one again."

David folded his arms against his chest and settled back in his chair. "But it's not reading your work that I remember, Jake. It's reading *about* you." He paused a moment. "Didn't you used to work for some paper down south? *The Atlanta Constitution*, maybe?"

Jake's smile faded. He felt his insides tighten into a knot, just as they did every time someone brought up the *Constitution* and his fall from grace.

Four years earlier, his wife, Alyssa—a pampered little heiress not all that unlike the one seated next to him, Jake forcefully reminded himself—had kicked him to the curb of her penthouse apartment once the novelty of their one-year marriage had worn off. Jake had never seen the breakup coming; hell, he'd never even suspected she was seeing another man until the day she'd told him that she was leaving him for some jet-setting oil tycoon from Houston.

Jake had been devastated, and he'd thrown himself into his work in an effort to hide the pain. The only problem was, he'd pushed for publication on a story about a favorite Georgia charity being used as a front for laundering drug money before verification of all the facts had been obtained. It'd been a mistake.

A big mistake.

After the story broke, his source had disappeared and the *Constitution* had been slapped with a multimillion-dollar lawsuit. With no way to prove the story, the paper had had to recant the charges and settle out of court. Jake had been sacked and had left Georgia in disgrace. It had taken him months to find another job, and then he'd been forced to work for a tabloid. He'd been making his slow crawl back from career oblivion ever since.

Jake eyed the still-smiling senator, who was holding court with his well-wishers on the dais.

Blowing the lid on McNichols's campaign hanky-panky ought to be just the story to put Jake back on top as a serious journalist.

"Yeah, I used to work for the *Constitution*," Jake said, breaking open the roll. He dipped his knife into the softened pad of butter on his bread plate and smeared it across a piece of the roll. "Who knows? I might even work for them again someday . . . provided they offered me enough money."

"Good evening, ladies and gentlemen," came the fund-raiser chairperson's booming voice seconds later from the podium. "One honest man *can* make a difference, and Todd McNichols is that man!"

A round of thunderous applause filled the ballroom. As if on cue, a couple of the red balloons lining the rafters began to make a slow descent.

Nice touch, Jake thought sarcastically, setting the pieces of dinner roll back down on his plate next to his untouched salad.

McNichols stood and started to wave. Also as if on cue, one of the senator's campaign workers in the back of the room jumped to his feet, initiating a standing ovation that was spreading like wildfire from table to table.

Still waving to the crowd, McNichols walked

over to the podium. The chairperson stepped aside and began to applaud as well.

"Thank you," McNichols murmured into the microphone. The applause grew louder. He turned and motioned for his parents to join him. They were a well-dressed couple in their early sixties, and wide, happy smiles covered their faces. They waved to everyone in the room.

McNichols turned toward Jake's table and extended his hand. "Maggie?"

Jake felt his insides go cold. His gaze shot toward Maggie. She'd gone slightly pale and was oblivious of him. Oblivious of everything, it seemed.

"Please?" McNichols entreated. He motioned for her to join him.

For a moment Jake was certain she was going to decline McNichols's request. Then she stood, reaching for her black beaded evening bag. She slid its thin metal strap onto her shoulder and slowly walked over to the podium. McNichols gave her a kiss on her cheek—the applause level in the ballroom increased a few decibels—then he slid his arm possessively around her waist and waved to the crowd. The inference about their relationship was impossible to miss.

So Maggie Thorpe was Senator McNichols's girlfriend, Jake thought coldly, trying to absorb the new information. No wonder Kingfisher had warned Maggie that McNichols wouldn't like her smuggling a tabloid reporter into the fund-raiser.

Although why she'd done so—and why she'd tried to pass him off as her date—was still as much a mystery to Jake now as it had been when she'd done it.

Jake tossed his linen napkin onto the table in disgust and rose to his feet just as the waiter came by with the main course. Skirting the food cart, Jake shouldered his way out of the room as the applause began to swell.

Hell, he'd wasted enough time for one night on a spoiled little debutante out looking for a new adventure. He'd come to this party hoping to find even more dirt to toss on McNichols's political coffin.

And it was high time Jake started looking for it.

Maggie wasn't sure just whom she was angrier with, Todd, for announcing to a roomful of overly enthusiastic campaign supporters—and one devastatingly handsome tabloid reporter out on a mission to derail Todd's political campaign—that they were the hottest item since Bogie and Bacall, or herself, for having given Todd that erroneous impression in the first place.

Stepping into the elevator, Maggie muttered another curse—she'd been mumbling a rather inventive string of epithets under her breath ever since she'd left the ballroom five minutes earlier—and punched in the button for the tenth floor. The elevator doors slowly closed and the car began its ascent.

Okay, so she'd gone out with Todd a couple of times. He'd needed a date for some campaign-related parties that he'd had to attend, and her father—blast him!—had suggested her as a stand-in. In appreciation, Todd had taken her to dinner at her favorite restaurant. While he had given her a kiss when he'd dropped her off that night, there had been absolutely no chemistry, no sparks, no anything between them. It had been like kissing an affectionate older brother.

She'd never thought again about the kiss or about Todd. Even if he was, as her father liked to point out, Ivy League–school handsome, had a brilliant political future ahead of him—Jake's threats to the contrary notwithstanding—and was probably the most eligible bachelor in the whole state of California.

As far as Maggie was concerned, Todd McNichols was also the most boring bachelor in the whole state . . . maybe even most of the western hemisphere.

The elevator pinged and the doors slid open. Maggie stepped out and started down the long, empty hall toward her room.

She'd speak with Todd later that night, she decided, digging into her evening bag for her key card—provided she could get him away from Raymond Kingfisher long enough to have a private conversation. She had no desire to hurt Todd, but she had to set him straight about their relationship, or, rather, their lack of one. She'd catch an early flight back to San Francisco the next morning.

There was another fund-raiser scheduled in San Diego two days away on Saturday night, which she now had no intention of attending. She'd put in an appearance at four of Todd's fund-raisers already—and one of them had been enough to bore her to tears. Then she'd averted a PR disaster with Jake and Raymond in the linen closet, only to have to suffer through Todd's romantic fantasies on the podium a short time later.

In her estimation, she'd more than done her duty for dear old Dad, and more than earned that sizable contribution for Pet Haven.

Maggie slowed when she reached her room at the end of the hallway. Directly opposite her door was Todd's two-bedroom suite . . . which was another thing that annoyed her, now that she thought about it.

When she'd checked into the hotel that afternoon, she'd assumed their room arrangements had been just an odd coincidence; now she was beginning to suspect it was due to some kind of amorous conspiracy orchestrated by Todd.

She muttered a curse again and started to slide the key card into the door. That's when a dull thud, followed by a muffled curse, sounded from the direction of Todd's suite. It was as though someone had bumped into a piece of furniture, and had been none too happy about it either.

Maggie glanced at the door to Todd's room, which she now noticed was standing slightly ajar.

Frowning, she took a step closer, doubting that housekeeping was working so late. She heard the sounds of rustling papers coming from inside the suite. They were the same kinds of sounds a burglar might make if he were rifling through the place— or the kind of sounds that a determined tabloid reporter might make when he was hot on the trail of a nonexistent story.

She started to grin.

Jake, she thought, feeling more pleased by the realization than she probably should have been.

She slipped her key card back into her purse. She knew it was he. She could feel it in her bones.

Before she could talk herself out of it, Maggie quietly pushed the door open and slipped into the suite, closing the door softly behind her.

The suite was composed of two bedrooms leading off a central living room; Todd was using the spare bedroom as his temporary campaign headquarters. As she suspected, Jake was in the extra bedroom now, squatting down on the floor, carefully scavenging through the wastebasket.

With his hair tumbling rakishly across his brow and his expression one of intense concentration, he looked for all the world like a sexier—and much better dressed—Indiana Jones carefully perusing some ancient documents while on the hunt for a fabled lost city.

Her grin deepened. "Some date you turned out

to be, Jake Wilder," she teased. "The minute my back was turned, you bailed on me."

Jake jumped, letting go with another expletive and nearly toppling the wastebasket onto its side.

"Was it the company?" she asked, walking toward him. "Or the fact that you just couldn't bear to face one of those stringy chicken dinners?"

"It was simple facts, Ms. Thorpe," Jake said in a voice so cold, it bordered on the frigid.

He dropped the sheaf of discarded campaign memorabilia back into the wastebasket and stood.

He wasn't returning her smile either, she noticed with dismay. In fact, the thick covering of ice seemed to be back in his Arctic blue eyes for good this time. As for that impossible-to-resist southern charm he'd been plying her with a short time before in the linen closet, well, it might have never even existed.

"I've got a story to write," he said.

She felt her smile fade. "Is that really all that matters to you? Getting your story?"

He shrugged. "What else is there?"

"I guess if you have to ask, there's really no point in my telling you."

She stopped a few inches away from him, standing close enough to feel the sudden tension rising off his muscled body, standing close enough, too, for the clean, masculine scent of his aftershave to overpower her senses, making her go slightly weak in the knees. She felt her breath catch in her throat.

"So just what is this big story of yours anyway?"

she asked, irritated that he could be standing so close to her and apparently not feel the same attraction that she felt for him. "And just what were you hoping to find in Todd's wastebasket that you could possibly *bury* him with?"

"No comment."

"Look, Jake," she said, "I've tried to be as nice about this as I possibly can, but I'm afraid that I just can't let you continue . . ."

Maggie's voice trailed off as she heard someone begin to insert a key card into the door lock in the other room. Her gaze flew toward the living room and then back to Jake. One glance told her that he'd heard the sound and knew what it meant.

She knew that it wasn't Todd coming back early—when she'd left the ballroom, the fundraiser had been in high gear, and Todd wouldn't very likely leave until he'd shaken every hand and tried to empty every pocket in the room. Her guess was that it was either Kingfisher or hotel security. Perhaps both. Either way, it meant trouble.

Unless she came up with some explanation—and a good one too—in about ten seconds or so for why she and Jake were in Todd's hotel suite, that scandal she'd been hoping to avoid for the sake of her father would erupt right there in her face.

Jake took a step toward the window and stopped, swearing bitterly beneath his breath. She could have told him he was only wasting his time. There was no balcony, and even if the windows did open, they led to nowhere except for a ten-floor drop.

"Kiss me," Maggie said, moving closer to him.

Jake swirled. "What?"

The word came out in a half-croak, as though he thought her suggestion was far worse than their impending danger.

She ran her hands up his chest—a strongly muscular chest, she was quick to notice as her hands slid over the smooth silk fabric of his dinner jacket. She linked her fingers around his neck.

"Kiss me," she said again, pulling him toward her just as she heard the door to the living room open.

Jake resisted for a moment longer, then his lips brushed lightly over hers—once, twice, in fact—before finally capturing them in the most toe-curlingly, heart-poundingly wonderful kiss she'd ever experienced in her entire twenty-seven years. His lips were firm yet soft, and they moved with a deliberate leisureliness over her mouth that left her craving more of him.

Much more.

She felt his hands slowly glide around her waist, sending shivers of anticipation cascading around her as he reached her buttocks. Then he pulled her closer against the hard length of his body. She started to relax, started to mold herself against him and, for an all-too-intoxicatingly brief moment, eagerly returned his kiss. Almost forgetting, in fact, that the kiss was just supposed to be a smoke screen and nothing more.

"Very funny, Ms. Thorpe," Raymond Kingfisher snarled from the doorway a second later, sending her crashing back to reality. "Unfortunately, I'm not the least bit amused."

THREE

Maggie slowly eased herself out of Jake's arms, not all that certain if her suddenly wobbly knees would support her weight or not when she let him go. She felt as if she'd just taken a quick spin on the world's most gravity-defying roller coaster: Her heart was pounding, her stomach was still turning flipflops, and she couldn't seem to catch her breath no matter how hard she tried.

She glanced up at Jake.

Fortunately, she wasn't the only one feeling slightly dazed by it all. Jake appeared to have taken the same emotionally dizzying ride she had.

The only difference was, with his flushed cheeks and passion-flecked gaze he looked like he'd gone for an extra spin or two around the track.

Good, she thought, feeling inordinately pleased by the discovery. *Very good.*

Unable to mask her triumphant smile, Maggie turned around.

"Raymond!"

She wondered briefly if she sounded as out of sorts in reality as she'd planned on pretending to be only moments before.

"I'm sorry," she went on breathlessly. "We, ah, didn't hear you come in."

"I gathered as much."

Raymond's thin lips were tightly pressed in rigid disapproval. His beady, reptilelike eyes slowly raked over them, moving from the top of their heads to the soles of their feet, making it abundantly clear that he didn't like what he saw one bit.

Rather than demand an explanation as to why they were using Todd's temporary campaign headquarters as their own private lover's lane, Raymond just calmly walked over to the oak writing table near the wall and lifted the telephone receiver.

"This is Raymond Kingfisher in Senator Mc-Nichols's room," he said a moment later. "I need to speak with someone in security. We've had a break-in."

Maggie groaned. "Raymond, wait. I can explain. Honestly."

Jake muttered another curse, clenching his hands into fists. "Put down the phone, Kingfisher," he growled in a voice as rough as gravel. "Don't make an even bigger ass out of yourself than you already are."

Jake started to move past her, but she stopped

him by clamping her hand onto his upper arm and giving it a gentle squeeze.

Their gazes met. Maggie could feel the coiled tension radiating from Jake's body. She didn't blame him for wanting to take a more aggressive stance. She'd wanted to punch Raymond's lights out herself on more than one occasion, but somehow she didn't think that now, when he was threatening them with probable arrest, was the appropriate time to act on the impulse.

"What Jake is trying to say," she said, turning back to face Raymond, "is that you should think—really think—about what you're doing here before you take any action."

Raymond could have been carved from stone for all the notice he paid her.

"I mean, do you really want the entire state to read all about this on the front page of tomorrow's *Sentinel*?" she asked. "Just think how it would look, Raymond. Mere minutes after Todd and I were waving to his throngs of supporters downstairs, you find me making out with another man in Todd's room."

She felt Jake start to relax. Raymond, however, started to look positively nervous.

As well he should.

This was Todd's first all-out run for United States senator. Two years earlier he'd been elected to the position in an interim election held to fill the vacancy created when long-time Senator Dan Newman had been elected governor. The latest poll figures that Maggie had seen had Todd easily winning his bid for a four-year term, but a scandal—even the suggestion of a scandal—could just as easily turn the tide of public sentiment in the opposite direction, especially since his opponent was gaining support in some of the more traditionally conservative counties.

"Think of all those nasty questions Todd will be bombarded with for weeks after," Maggie went on, pressing home her advantage. "About me and him . . . and about Jake and me . . . in Todd's own bedroom while he was downstairs campaigning for the senate. Politically, it could be very embarrassing for him."

For that matter, it could be very embarrassing for her, especially since none of it was particularly true.

"Why take the risk of damaging Todd's hopes for reelection?" she asked. "After all, we could straighten out this misunderstanding rather easily if you'd just give us a chance to explain."

A few seconds passed. Raymond's frown deepened into a scowl.

"Yes, I'm still here," he snapped into the receiver.

Maggie held her breath.

"No, that won't be necessary," he said. "It appears to have been a false alarm. I'll advise if the situation changes though. Thank you."

Maggie exhaled. She released Jake's arm. "Thank you, Raymond."

Raymond slowly dropped the receiver back into the handset and folded his arms against his chest.

"I'm listening," he said.

"Okay. Now, I admit that this—" She motioned to Jake and then back to herself. "Well, I could see how this might look to you. I mean, first you find us in the linen closet, sharing a bottle of wine, and now you find us sharing kisses in Todd's room . . . it's kind of hard to believe it's just our first date, isn't it?"

She offered Raymond what she'd been told was a delightfully winsome smile. He just stared back at her, decidedly unimpressed.

"Is there some point you're trying to make here, Ms. Thorpe?" he asked coldly.

"Well, of course there is, Raymond," she said. "I'm trying to tell you that Jake and I had a very innocent reason for being in Todd's room."

The only problem was that she couldn't for the life of her think of just what that reason might have been.

"Just tell him the truth, Maggie," Jake suggested.

"The truth?"

She glanced up at him as if he'd just lost his mind. Telling the truth was probably the last thing they should do right then.

"The truth *would* be a refreshing change, Ms. Thorpe," Raymond said dryly.

Jake smiled, but it was a dangerous sort of smile, she decided. The kind she imagined the wolf might have given Little Red Riding Hood right before he fed her that line about his being her beloved grandmother.

"And the truth is that Maggie didn't break into the senator's room," Jake said, keeping his gaze locked on Raymond. "Nor did she help me break in, which is what you're probably thinking. We found the door standing ajar, and she decided to play amateur detective."

"That's impossible," Raymond said.

"But it's true," Maggie said, picking up the thread of the story and deciding to run with it. "Of course, when I pointed out the open door to Jake, he immediately insisted we contact hotel security."

"It seemed the sensible thing to do," Jake said nonchalantly. "After all, it could've been another Watergate scandal in the making, or something worse."

Maggie nodded. "Yes, but I insisted we investigate . . . for Todd's sake, I mean."

"Ms. Thorpe, the door couldn't possibly have been standing open," Raymond said again, more wearily this time.

"Luckily, there was no one here," Maggie said, ignoring him. "Nothing seemed to be missing or out of place either, so we just assumed that Todd must have forgotten to close the door completely when he went downstairs. That can happen sometimes if you don't firmly pull it closed behind you. Anyway, Jake and I were just about to leave when, ah, that other thing happened."

Raymond eyed her strangely. "What other thing?"

Maggie glanced up at Jake again. He cocked an eyebrow at her. She couldn't resist a grin.

"Well, I believe that we'd been standing sort of where we are right now," she said, keeping her gaze linked with Jake's.

Amusement began to dance deep within the depths of his azure-colored eyes . . . along with the smoldering embers of that erotic fire storm they'd nearly unleashed a short time before.

"Jake started telling me how positively gorgeous I looked," she went on, feeling her stomach do another little flipflop. "About how he'd been fantasizing all night long about kissing me."

As long as they were trying to sell a few fairy tales, she figured she might as well include one for herself. Having Jake Wilder relentlessly pursue her with sweetly worded lies had a certain irresistible appeal.

"Almost before I knew what was happening," she said, feeling herself blush, "Jake had swept me into his arms, and, well, I guess you know the rest, Raymond."

Jake's smile deepened until she was certain that dimple in his chin was winking at her.

"Actually, technically, Maggie darlin'," he said, taking a step closer.

Her heart fluttered widly in her chest.

"I think you were the one who kissed me," he said.

His soft drawl was so seductive, it could make a woman shiver with sensual delight.

Well, this woman anyway, Maggie decided, feeling goose bumps start to ripple along her arms.

"Not that I'm complaining, mind you," he added with a grin.

He raised his hand and slowly rubbed his thumb along the curve of her cheek, sending another tingling round of goose bumps sliding along her flesh.

Her breath caught in her throat. Her abdominal muscles began to tighten.

"I, ah, just wanted to set the record straight," he murmured.

She felt herself begin to flush. "But I kissed you first only because I thought I might be old and gray before you ever got around to it," she said softly.

Jake laughed. The sound was low and husky, and it spun her imagination even further out of control.

"Not a chance," he said, leaning closer.

"This is all very interesting, I'm sure, but you couldn't have found the senator's door open," Raymond said, refusing to be conned by their little sideshow or anything else. "It was locked. I know, because I checked it myself before we left."

Jake's hand dropped back to his side. "Then you obviously need to be more thorough in executing your responsibilities around here," he said, glancing back at Raymond.

"Exactly, Raymond," she piped in, amazed that she could sound relatively normal despite the liquid heat still racing through her veins. "Why, if Jake and I hadn't walked by, who knows what could've happened?"

And if she and Jake weren't there with Raymond now, the possibilities were even more intriguing.

Raymond scowled. "This is ridiculous," he snarled. "You're both lying, and not very well either. Unfortunately, I don't wish to cause the senator any of the . . . public embarrassment . . . that you mentioned earlier, so without any proof to back up my suspicions, I've got no choice but to let the whole matter drop."

Raymond gave a dramatic sweep of his hand toward the door. "I'm sure that you can both find your way out," he added sarcastically.

"No problem," Maggie said.

Then, grabbing Jake's hand, she made a mad rush toward the living room door before Raymond had a chance to change his mind. Once outside in the hallway, she collapsed against the wall, not sure if she should burst out laughing or strangle Jake with her bare hands.

"You, Jake Wilder, owe me a drink," Maggie decreed, releasing his hand. "Something emotionally soothing in a tall, cool glass. Definitely a double."

Jake grinned. "Give me a call next time you're in L.A., Maggie darlin', and you're on."

He turned to head for the elevators.

"Unh-unh," she said, bolting after him. "Not so fast."

She linked her arm with his and fell into step beside him, matching him stride for stride.

"You also owe me an explanation," she said. "And I've got no intention of letting you leave this hotel until I get both."

"So just what is it that you think Todd has been doing? Cheating on his income tax? Hiring an undocumented alien to detail his limo? What?"

Maggie asked Jake the questions moments after they'd been served their wine in the hotel's dimly lit piano bar. Her request for information was a reasonable one. Only problem was, he was still uncertain just how much—if anything at all—he should reveal to her.

Jake glanced around the crowded lounge. As far as he could tell, none of the intimate groupings of white wicker chairs padded with plump floral-colored cushions were unoccupied—some people had even carted in chairs from the adjacent lobby. The pianist was on a break, so the room hummed with the sounds of laughter and lively conversations. Although Jake wasn't certain—they were seated near the back of the bar, and a large potted fern blocked most of his view—he suspected that some of the more boisterous people sitting next to the piano were fellow reporters.

And the last thing he figured he needed was for

them to hear about his scoop before it was published in the *Sentinel.*

"This isn't the place to have that kind of conversation," he said quietly. "Too many people. Too much chance of someone overhearing us."

Maggie glanced around her. Then she scooted her wicker chair around the glass-and-chrome table until it was next to his.

She leaned toward him. Their knees made contact again, this time sending an intoxicating warmth sluicing through his bloodstream that was far more potent than any beverage they might have served in the bar. Then the soft floral scent of her perfume floated around him too, invading his senses, overpowering his resolve to keep her at a safe emotional distance from here on out.

"Is this better?" she asked.

Her voice stroked his ego like a gentle caress.

"Or should we drop our napkins at the count of three and meet under the table?" she suggested.

He took a long swallow of wine, trying to ignore the pressure of her evening gown's black beads against his thigh, and the tantalizing curve of her breasts visible through the form-fitting dress each time he glanced at her.

"You're enjoying yourself, aren't you?" he murmured huskily.

"Immensely." Her eyes were sparkling with mischief and the promise of more erotically charged mayhem to come. "But seriously, Jake," she said, "after all we've been through together tonight, I do think you owe me an explanation, don't you?"

"You already have an explanation. I'm working on a story."

"Uh-huh. About Todd. Something that will bury him. I just want to know what that something is."

She leaned closer until their shoulders touched. A strand of her honey-gold hair brushed against his chin. He drew a sharp breath. His heart started to pound.

"Now, stop being cagey," she said. "Give."

"Cagey? Me?"

"With a capital C."

He laughed. "I'm not trying to avoid answering you. Honest. It's just that now isn't the appropriate time and place to have this discussion, that's all."

"Uh-huh. Look, I know exactly how oblivious to the rest of the world you single-minded obsessive types can be when you lock your sights on a goal. Why, before he saw the error of his ways, my father used to be as committed to running Thorpe Industries and orchestrating his political campaigns as you are with getting your story. So don't you think for a single, solitary moment, Jake Wilder, that I'm going to let you get away with ignoring me and my question."

She leaned in closer still.

"Give," she said again.

She was wasting her talents on him, he decided. She could work for the government as a high-level interrogator of enemy agents. Jake doubted if any man alive could withstand her undeniably sexy charms for too long without succumbing and giving her any damn thing she wanted.

"Okay, okay," he said, taking another swallow of wine. "Basically, I think your boyfriend is a slimebag." He slid his glass back on the table.

"He's not my boyfriend."

He glanced at her. "Oh?"

She shook her head. "Not even close."

He smiled. "Does he know that? I ask only because I got the distinct impression at the fundraiser tonight that McNichols thinks otherwise."

Maggie gave him an overly dramatized sigh. "Don't remind me."

She slowly traced a fingertip along the rim of her wineglass. Jake watched her for a moment, hypnotized by the sensual movement of her hand, fantasizing that her finger was drawing that same slow circle on his bare chest . . . just as his own hands were leisurely discovering every voluptuous curve of her body now discreetly hidden from his view by her evening gown.

His mouth went suddenly dry. He reached for his wine goblet and downed its contents.

"We went out a couple of times," she said softly. "Strictly casual, nothing serious. I thought he understood we were just friends. . . ." She shrugged. "I plan to straighten it out later tonight."

"Before Kingfisher does, you mean?" he asked,

knowing that his voice had gone a little rougher around the edges than he'd have liked.

She glanced up and met his gaze.

"My guess is he's going to tell McNichols that we were in his room tonight," Jake went on. "And I'm also guessing that Todd isn't going to like hearing that his . . . friend . . . is running around kissing tabloid reporters." Because if Maggie had been his woman, Jake damn sure wouldn't have liked it.

She grinned. "Desperate times sometimes call for desperate actions."

He felt his body grow harder still. "I guess they do at that."

"And it was a tough job too," she said breathlessly. "Kissing you, I mean."

She gave him that naughty smile of hers again, the one that played absolute hell with his emotional defenses. It fired his imagination, kicking his libido into overdrive in nothing flat, making his pulse race and his blood run hotter than molten steel.

"I'm, ah, sorry it was so rough on you," he said, knowing he sounded equally as breathless.

Before he could stop himself, he leaned over and stroked her cheek with the back of his hand— her skin felt smoother and softer than anything he'd ever touched before. The muscles in his lower abdomen began to constrict.

"Having to kiss me, I mean," he said.

He slowly glided his hand up to her hair and rubbed a silky strand between his thumb and forefinger. Liquid heat raced through his veins. His arousal started to strain against his trousers.

She drew a slow, ragged breath. "Well . . . maybe it wasn't that bad."

"No?"

She gave him another smile.

"No," she said. "And I might even be willing to suffer through the experience a second time . . . provided the cause was important enough, of course."

He grinned. "Why, that's awfully sporting of you, Ms. Thorpe."

"I think so," she murmured.

He glided his hand around the curve of her neck, luxuriating in the feel of her silky hair against his fingers. He tilted her head back. Her gaze locked with his. The message in her hazel eyes was unmistakable just then. She wanted him. Almost as badly as he wanted her. In fact, the sexual sparks flying between them were enough to set off a virtual fire storm, the kind of fire storm that could destroy a man's sanity with very little effort.

He squeezed his eyes closed and took a deep breath. "What the hell am I supposed to do with you, Maggie Thorpe?" he whispered softly. "You're just so—"

"Positively gorgeous," she suggested, using the phrase she'd attributed to him earlier in their confrontation with Kingfisher.

He sighed. "Exactly," he murmured, opening

his eyes. "And you were right . . . I had been fantasizing all night long about kissing you."

Something told him that he would probably continue thinking those kinds of thoughts about her for quite some time to come.

"Funny you should say that, Mr. Wilder . . ."

Her voice sounded as tattered and frayed as his willpower was quickly becoming.

She grabbed the lapel of his jacket and pulled him a little closer.

"I've, ah, been having the same fantasies myself about you," she said.

Her lips slowly parted in a smile. He knew she was waiting for him to kiss her.

And, God, how he wanted to give in to the craving too, Jake thought. How he wanted to pull her close to him and kiss her until the hunger, the need, no longer burned inside him. How he wanted to kiss her until she lay limp and boneless and utterly content in his arms. He wanted it so badly, it was killing him.

He removed her hand from his jacket and slowly pulled away.

"Only . . . I've . . . got no intention of following through on any of my fantasies tonight," he said huskily. "As tempting as all this is, I'm afraid that I'm just not interested in becoming another addition to your trophy case—like that poor sap Senator McNichols. Or Charlie Darnell before him."

Maggie blinked at him, looking as if she'd just

been inexplicably shoved into the deep end of a pool.

"What are you talk—my trophy case?"

"I'm talking about us," he said. "Or, rather, how there isn't going to be any us. I'm letting you know, Maggie darlin', that I've had my fill of pampered little debutantes . . . and I'm just not interested in getting involved with another one."

Jake tossed a couple of bills onto the table and left the bar without so much as a backward glance. He had no choice but to leave and to leave fast, because one good look at his face—and certain other parts of his anatomy—and Maggie would know he was lying through his teeth when he said he wasn't interested in her.

If he spent one more second gazing into Maggie's eyes, feeling her silky hair rustle beneath his fingers, feeling her knee pressed intimately against his, Jake would have likely hauled her back upstairs to her room to follow through on half a dozen or so of both their fantasies.

Damn the probable consequences.

One hour and another glass of Chablis later, Maggie returned to her room, still feeling as if she'd been dealt a sucker punch.

Who did Jake Wilder think he was? she asked herself for probably the hundredth time since he'd bolted from the bar. He had practically seduced her with that bad-boy grin of his and then said he didn't want to become another addition to her trophy case! How dare he talk to her that way when she'd bailed him out of not one, but two tight squeezes without receiving so much as a thank-you in return?

Worse still, how dare he tell her he wasn't interested in her, when her lips were still yearning for another kiss? When her heart could still race and her stomach still turn a few hundred flipflops from just remembering his smile?

Maggie glanced over at Todd's suite as she stood in front of her door. She wearily raked her fingers through her hair, and supposed there was no point in putting off her little chat with Todd any longer. It had to be done, and the sooner she got it over with, the sooner she could put this whole mess behind her.

She slipped the metal strap of her evening bag back onto her shoulder and walked over to his door. She gave it a light tap.

"Todd?" she called softly. She could hear muffled voices coming from inside.

When she got no answer, she turned the knob, pushed the door open, and walked inside. Raymond Kingfisher and another man she couldn't quite see were talking in the next room.

She took a step closer, wondering if Todd was with them or if he was still downstairs somewhere, campaigning the night away.

". . . problem is he's obviously smitten with her," the other man was saying.

Maggie could see him through the doorway now. It was Karl Vedder, a lobbyist for the timber industry, whom she'd met in San Francisco the week before. Vedder was a large, heavyset man in his late forties who never seemed to be without his cheap cigars, one of which he was smoking then.

"I know," Raymond said. "And Maggie Thorpe is definitely a liability to the senator's political future. I'm planning to talk to him about her later tonight, advise him to distance himself from her as quickly as he can for the sake of the campaign."

Maggie smiled. *Good idea, Raymond*, she thought. And maybe if he hurried, she wouldn't have to have that little heart-to-heart with Todd.

"The problem is it may already be too late," Raymond went on. "She smuggled that reporter from the *Sentinel*—Jake Wilder's his name—into the fund-raiser before I could stop her. I later caught them up here, snooping around. I doubt if Wilder found anything though."

"Well, he'd damn well better not have," Vedder said.

The acrid smell of cigar smoke floated out to Maggie. She wrinkled her nose in distaste.

"We've invested too much money in Todd's campaign to have him lose the election over a nosy reporter. Hell, the Landerman bill is scheduled to be one of the first items of business once the new session begins."

Maggie began to feel slightly queasy. She had a funny feeling she now knew what Jake's big story was. Todd McNichols, who'd been campaigning for months about the need for political reform, was selling his senatorial votes to the highest bidder.

She was vaguely familiar with the Landerman bill, mostly because she'd heard her father speak of it. She knew it had something to do with restricting the additional harvesting of old-growth trees in the Pacific Northwest; the timber industry had successfully blocked its passage during the last session, but it was generally expected to pass through Congress and hit the Senate early the next year.

"You promised me some support, and by damn—"

"And the senator will deliver that support, I assure you," Raymond murmured reassuringly. "I'm just not sure what to do about Wilder, that's all."

Vedder took a long draw on his cigar. "Buy him off."

"Impossible."

"Then eliminate him," Vedder said. "Arrange an accident, something that can't be traced back to us. I don't care what you do, as long as you get rid of him. Permanently."

Maggie gasped. Feeling her blood turn to ice water, she took a step backward and rammed into the sofa, shoving it back across the floor several inches. She'd made enough noise to alert half the city to her presence in the room.

Not bothering to see if Raymond and Vedder had heard her or not, Maggie swirled and headed out the door as fast as her legs could take her. One of the metal links of her purse strap got caught on the door handle to Todd's room, tugging her evening bag off her shoulder as she ran. Her purse hit the floor with a thud. She didn't dare stop long enough to retrieve it though, and raced down the hallway to the stairwell door.

Jake was right, she thought, taking the steps two at a time. Todd McNichols was a slimebag.

She only hoped that she could find Jake before Todd's goons did, and tell him so.

FOUR

"What the hell do you mean, Maggie Thorpe has disappeared?"

Jake snarled the question at Liebowitz and Brenner after they'd dropped their bombshell in the *Sentinel*'s newsroom at a few minutes past eight the following morning.

"Just that," drawled Sandy Brenner, a stockily built redhead in his late thirties. He motioned toward the small color television that he and several other staffers were gathered around, drinking their coffee.

"America's favorite deb has disappeared," he said. "Vanished into thin air. Dropped out of sight."

"Taken the proverbial powder."

The last comment came from Brenner's long-time partner, Bob Liebowitz, a slender forty-year-old with receding brown hair.

"And just when we needed a good headline for

tomorrow's edition too," Liebowitz added, grinning. "Bless that woman."

Laughter rippled through the newsroom.

Jake scowled and pushed his way closer to the television set. A female reporter for the Channel Eight news team was giving a live report from outside the Universal Hilton. Jake turned up the volume.

". . . vanished sometime last night after the senator's fund-raiser here at the hotel," she was saying. "Miss Thorpe, who is the only child of San Francisco industrialist Peter Thorpe, a prominent political power broker, has been linked romantically with Senator McNichols for some time now. At a press conference earlier this morning, the senator appeared visibly shaken by Miss Thorpe's disappearance."

The reporter wasn't exaggerating either, Jake decided, as a disheveled and obviously worried-looking McNichols flashed into view. McNichols issued a brief statement, echoing the sketchy details given by the reporter, then he concluded with a request that anyone with information on Maggie's whereabouts please contact either his office or the police.

So Maggie really had vanished, Jake thought, feeling uneasy by the realization. He knew it was no use trying to convince himself that Liebowitz and Brenner's theory was correct, that Maggie's sudden disappearance was just another one of those infamous Thorpe exploits the papers loved so much. If she'd decided to cut her stay at the Hilton short—say, because of anything he might have said to her in the hotel bar, for example—she'd have taken her luggage with her, or at least her evening bag, which contained her identification and credit cards. According to McNichols, her purse was found in the hallway outside her room . . . as though she'd dropped it, but had been leaving the hotel in such a hurry that she hadn't had time to retrieve it.

Or she hadn't been allowed to, Jake thought, feeling chilled to the bone.

The telephone started to ring. Brenner reached over and snagged the receiver nearest the television.

"Brenner," he mumbled. "Sure, hold on." He lowered the receiver. "It's for you, Wilder. Sounds like your landlady."

Jake took the receiver, keeping his gaze locked on the television screen. "Sorry, Mrs. Quebral," he said. "This isn't a good time to chat right now."

Victoria Quebral was a petite lady in her late fifties whose only hobbies, as far as Jake knew, were acting as his surrogate mother and talking about her two Siamese cats.

"And who wants to chat?" she asked huffily. "I'm calling to find out why you didn't tell me your sister was coming out for a visit."

"My sister?" He frowned. "I'm afraid I don't know what you're—"

"She arrived here about ten minutes ago, asking

for you," she said, interrupting him. "I wasn't sure what to do with her, so I let her into your apartment. The poor thing looked like she was dead on her feet . . . and with those high heels of hers, it's no wonder."

"Wait a minute," he said. "Are you saying that you let some strange woman into my—"

The hairs began to prickle at the back of his neck. *The poor thing looked like she was dead on her feet . . . and with those high heels of hers, it's no wonder.*

No, it couldn't be, he told himself.

Liebowitz and Brenner started to eye him curiously. Jake turned away.

"Ah, Mrs. Quebral," Jake said, lowering his voice. "What does she look like? My sister, I mean."

"Don't you know what your own sister looks like, Jake?" she asked in disbelief.

"I come from a big family. I've got a couple of them."

Both were happily married brunettes living in Georgia with no plans to visit Southern California the last he heard.

"Well, she's blond and very beautiful," Mrs. Quebral said. "Like a young Grace Kelly—very elegant and sophisticated-looking, I mean. She was even dressed like she was on her way to some fancy ball."

Jake grinned. "Let me guess," he murmured. "Black beaded evening gown?"

"Why, yes," Mrs. Quebral said, sounding surprised. "How did you know?"

"Old family eccentricity," Jake said. "Thanks, Mrs. Q. I'm on my way."

Jake lived in an older though still fashionable section of Sherman Oaks, an upscale suburb of Los Angeles located in the southeastern San Fernando Valley. Luckily for him, when he pulled his black Honda Accord into the carport twenty minutes after their phone call, Mrs. Quebral wasn't outside in the flower-filled courtyard playing with her cats, so he was able to slip into his ground-floor one-bedroom apartment unnoticed.

It didn't take him long to find Maggie.

A hint of her expensive perfume still lingered in the living room. All he had to do was follow its alluring aroma down the hall and back to his bedroom like a moth being drawn straight into a flame.

She was lying on her side, navy blue and gray striped comforter pulled up to her neck, fast asleep. She was as beautiful as ever, he decided, even if she did look far too natural sleeping in his rumpled bed to suit his comfort level.

He stood in the doorway for a moment, torn between wanting to let her sleep and wanting to shake some answers out of her. Hell, she'd vanished into thin air nearly twelve hours earlier. The worst part was that he still didn't know what had happened, if anything, to cause her to take flight or why she'd decided to turn up on his doorstep, claiming to be his long-lost sister. All he knew for certain was that he was happy to see her.

Damn happy, in fact.

He smiled. With her eyelashes curved gently along her upper cheeks, and her long blond hair spread around her head like some golden halo, she looked as guileless as an angel. His gaze dropped to the evening gown, lacy brassiere, and crumpled silk hose lying discarded on the floor next to her expensive black velvet pumps.

Better make that a fallen angel, he decided with a grin, since she was apparently naked.

As though she had read his thoughts, Maggie murmured something in her sleep and rolled over, giving him a quick glimpse of a loose-fitting red and blue top. Okay, so she wasn't completely naked, he amended with a disappointed sigh. Before she'd tumbled into his bed, she'd apparently rummaged through his closet until she'd found his Ole Miss football jersey.

Oddly enough, though, knowing that she was wearing his clothes struck him as being even more erotic than if she'd climbed into his bed totally nude. Mostly because his imagination had damned little trouble picturing the large cotton jersey skimming the alluringly feminine curves of her body when she rolled over in her sleep. . . .

Or picturing that same fabric pulled tightly across her full, rounded breasts, and how they'd rise and fall with each breath she took . . .

Or feeling the jersey slide slowly upward as he glided his palm along her smooth, tanned legs in a gentle caress . . .

Or hearing her softly moan his name as his lips replaced his hands in their slow, thorough exploration of her body . . . touching, kissing, tasting every luscious inch of her until he'd finally had his fill.

His abdominal muscles started to constrict; his body began to tighten.

Damn.

What the devil was the matter with him? he wondered, forcing himself to take a deep, steadying breath. Just thinking about touching the woman was enough to arouse him to the point of near insanity. Heaven help him if he ever actually followed through on any of his fantasies where she was concerned. The chances were excellent that he wouldn't survive the resulting emotional onslaught.

"Maggie," he called out hoarsely. "Wake up."

She jerked awake, clutching the comforter close to her chest as she scrambled upright in bed. Her hair fell around her face in sleep-tossed disarray. Her eyes went wide with shock and fear.

He scowled, feeling like a jerk for having scared her out of her wits when the problem with his out-of-control libido was his, not hers.

"Hey, it's okay," he said, softer this time. "It's just me."

"Jake," she whispered.

Her voice was husky and colored with sleep, but there was no mistaking its edge of terror.

Then she sighed with relief. "Where have you been?" she asked, sounding a little annoyed with him. "Mrs. Quebral said she'd have you come right over. I tried to stay awake until you got here, but I was so tired."

"Where have *I* been?" He took a step into the bedroom. "You're the one they've got half the police force out looking for." And probably every reporter on the planet too, hoping to score an exclusive.

"I was so worried about you," she said, frowning up at him.

She kicked off the comforter and swung her long legs—they were as smooth and brown and perfectly curved as his imagination had pictured them—over the edge of the bed. The bottom of the jersey started to crawl up, giving him an even longer glimpse of her tanned thighs. He drew a sharp breath.

He told himself to look away, but his gaze seemed glued to the gentle curve of her upper legs . . . and to the swell of her unbound breasts straining against the soft cotton fabric of the football jersey. A surge of sensual heat swept over him, warming him straight through to his core, turning his earlier arousal into an almost painful aching need to reach out and touch her.

Yet he didn't move.

His heart started to pound. His mouth went dry. He swallowed hard and forced his gaze away from her.

"The first thing I did when I left the hotel last night was call the *Sentinel*," she went on, seemingly oblivious of the effect she had upon him.

She stood and started to pace around the room, moving from the walk-in closet on the left, around the king-size bed and over to the oak dresser on the right, and then back again.

"I asked them to find you, but they said they couldn't help me," she said. "All the guy who answered the phone knew was that you lived in the Valley somewhere. Do you have any idea how many *people* live in the San Fernando Valley?" she asked, glancing back at him.

She raked her fingers through her hair and kept pacing, not really expecting him to answer.

Good thing too. Jake didn't think he was capable of saying anything even approaching coherency.

"Why, there must have been dozens of J. Wilders listed in the telephone directory," she said. "They were strewn from Woodland Hills to West Hills to Granada Hills—just what is it with the city of Los Angeles and all these damned Hills anyway?"

He shook his head. "Maggie . . ."

"I was frantic," she said, her voice rising another octave. She hugged her arms against her chest. "I didn't have any cash for cab fare. The banks wouldn't open till morning—not that I could withdraw any money without my ID—and my parents are cruising down the Amazon with the closest phone about a million miles away from them or something. I was all *alone*." Her voice started to break. "I didn't know what to do—"

"Whoa, whoa," he said, moving closer to her.

He reached out and grabbed her elbow as she rounded the bed again, slowing her to a stop. Her face was etched with anxiety, her body tense.

All the same, the casual contact of his palm against her bare arm sent an electric thrill coursing through him, setting his nerve endings aflame and making his body grow harder still. Then the subtle scent of roses swirled around him again, throwing him even more emotionally off balance.

He felt himself flush. "Just . . . take a deep breath," he said, releasing her elbow. "Try to relax."

Deciding to take his own advice, Jake took a step back, stopping a good ten inches away from her. He tried to reassure himself that if he stayed some discreet distance away from her, it would somehow, magically, alleviate the need, the hunger, she was able to arouse in him with virtually no effort on her part at all.

Only problem was it didn't seem to work.

Hell, it wasn't even coming close.

"Now, tell me what was so important that you spent half the night looking for me," he said.

"I had to talk to you."

Her gaze locked with his. There were no mischievous lights dancing in her hazel eyes this time, only fear—a fear so stark, so heartrendingly real, it made his blood run cold.

She hugged herself again. "I didn't know who else to turn to," she added softly.

Jake felt something tighten inside his chest. "Why don't you start from the beginning," he said. "Tell me exactly what happened."

She took a deep breath, then sat back down on the edge of the bed as though she'd expended all the energy she'd had remaining in her bout of frenzied pacing. She pulled her legs up and tucked them underneath her.

"After . . . after you left the bar, I had another glass of wine," she said. She met his gaze again and slowly smiled. "To, ah, tell the truth, I was trying to figure out what I could have possibly done to make you change the way you did and start talking all that nonsense about my trophy case."

He felt himself flush again, but in embarrassment this time.

Her smile only seemed to grow wider.

"In fact, Mr. Wilder," she said in a teasing tone that sounded more like her usual self. "A girl's ego could take a real beating around you . . . if she thought you were really serious, that is."

"Maggie, I—"

She waved him quiet. "Anyway, when I got back to my room," she said, getting back down to business, "I decided to have a little talk with Todd. I wanted to set him straight before I flew back to San Francisco, only Todd wasn't in his room."

Jake took a deep breath, trying to force his own

thoughts back on track. "And I suppose Kingfisher was?" he asked, taking a wild guess.

She nodded. "He was talking with another man, Karl Vedder." She frowned. "Vedder's a lobbyist for the timber industry. Apparently, he's—"

"He's been contributing heavily to McNichols's campaign. Yeah, I know."

Jake had been tracking Vedder's involvement with McNichols for over five weeks now.

"Exactly what did you hear them say?" he asked.

She pushed her hair back from her forehead. Her hand started to tremble.

"That Todd's been selling his senatorial votes," she said. "And that you've been nosing around for proof, although Raymond didn't think you'd actually found any."

"Raymond's mistaken."

Jake had proof, or he would have once he received the packet of expense receipts he'd been promised by a contact at Vedder's D.C. office. Airline ticket stubs, hotel bills, records of restaurant and bar charges—they all proved beyond any possible doubt that Vedder had picked up the tab on several Caribbean excursions the good senator had taken over the past year.

Of course, by themselves they didn't prove that McNichols was selling his votes on key pieces of legislation. However, considering McNichols's campaign promise to outlaw the practice of elected officials receiving all-expense-paid vacations from special interests groups—and McNichols's position on several subcommittees overseeing the timber industry—Jake figured that McNichols would have a lot of explaining to do to his constituents come election day, which was less than two months away.

"What else did they say?" Jake asked.

The color slowly drained from Maggie's face, yet her gaze never wavered.

"Vedder said Raymond should arrange for you to have an accident," she said quietly. "Something that couldn't be traced back to them."

Jake went still.

"I, ah, guess I freaked when I heard it," she went on, dropping her gaze. She plucked at the edge of the comforter, then pulled it closer to her as though she felt chilled. "I tried to beat a hasty retreat from the suite and ended up crashing into a sofa." She gave a forced laugh. "It wasn't one of my better exits, believe me."

"Did Kingfisher see you?"

"I don't think so, but he has to have known it was me. I caught the strap of my evening bag on the door handle on my way out of the suite. I didn't have time to stop to retrieve my purse, so I just left it there."

That explained why Maggie's purse had supposedly been found in the hallway outside her room, although McNichols's spin doctors had changed the details of its discovery just enough to remove any possible link from the good senator to Maggie's sudden disappearance.

"Earlier you said something about how half the police force was out looking for me," she said. "Were you serious?"

Jake nodded. "McNichols reported you missing sometime last night. As far as I can tell, the police are treating it as a possible kidnapping. They're pulling out all the stops trying to find you."

She muttered a curse and gave the comforter another tug, bringing it up to her shoulders.

"McNichols held a press conference this morning," Jake went on, walking toward her. "He looked worried . . . my guess is that he's afraid of what you'll say once you talk to the police."

"Yeah, right."

He stopped beside the bed. "You should have gone to the police last night, Maggie, told them everything you'd overheard, instead of trying to find me."

"Uh-huh. And I suppose the police would've just marched right over there and rounded them all up."

"Possibly."

"Yeah, right," she muttered again. "The man's a United States senator, for crying out loud! He's respected by thousands, and he's a probable shoo-in for the November election."

"So?"

"*So?*"

She slumped back in bed, scowling.

"So, as you pointed out so charmingly to me last night, I've got something of an image problem.

Thanks to the *Sentinel*, everyone seems to think that I'm . . . what was it you called me again? Some kind of pampered little debutante?" Her scowl deepened. "The police would probably think I was either just exaggerating or outright lying about what I'd heard, and that I'd disappeared just for the sake of getting some media attention."

Jake sighed wearily and rubbed his eyes. Maggie had a point. Without corroborating evidence to back up her allegations of murder plots and political corruption, she would probably be laughed out of the precinct house . . . if not arrested for making a nuisance of herself.

Not that Jake himself would likely fare any better if he went forward with what he knew without the evidence from Vedder's office to back up the allegations about McNichols's cozy involvement with the timber industry. Thanks to the Atlanta debacle, Jake knew he enjoyed even less credibility with authorities than Maggie probably did.

"What about your father?" he asked. "He'd believe you, wouldn't he? And if he went with you to the police, they'd have to listen to you."

"Yes, but unfortunately Father is incommunicado for the next two weeks, or weren't you paying attention to *anything* I said last night?"

He met her annoyed-looking gaze. Then he smiled again, softer this time.

"Oh, I was paying attention, Ms. Thorpe," he said, dropping his voice to a low murmur. "As I recall, I practically hung on your every word."

She arched an eyebrow, then the tension seemed to leave her slender body. She gave him a smile—the one she had that was so damned warmly inviting it almost bordered on the immoral, the one she had that melted his resolve like cubes of sugar in hot coffee, the one that he suspected they both knew he was utterly powerless to resist.

"Did you now?" she said huskily.

The mischievous lights in her hazel eyes started to sparkle and dance again. She sat up in bed, dropping the comforter to her waist and giving him another peek at the outline of her breasts through the jersey.

"Why don't you tell me about it, Mr. Wilder," she suggested, almost purring now. "Exactly how you hung on my words and all. Who knows? If I like how you say it, I might even be willing to forgive you for running out on me . . . twice."

A wave of sensual heat crashed around him again, making his breath catch in his throat. His abdominal muscles began to tighten.

He dropped his gaze.

"I . . . don't think now is the appropriate time for us to get sidetracked," he said hoarsely. "Not as long as McNichols is still out there . . . not as long as he poses a threat to your safety."

"Oh, get serious, darling," she said. "Todd wouldn't send his goons after me. And why should he? I've already told you that no one would believe anything I might say about him."

She reached up and wrapped her fingers firmly

around his forearm, then she pulled him down on the bed beside her before he could stop her.

His heart started to pound. Her fingertips felt as though they were scorching a path straight through the lightweight wool of his jacket to brand his skin with her touch.

"You're the one I'm worried about," she said softly, meeting his gaze. "I've been almost frantic. Why else do you think I would have spent all night chasing after you?"

"You were worried about *me*?"

His raw voice sounded skeptical, as though it had been a long time since anyone had cared enough to worry about his safety.

"More like absolutely terrified," Maggie said.

She kept her gaze locked with his, wondering briefly if she was foolishly endangering her already-fragile emotional defense system by staring so intently into his azure-colored eyes.

Wondering, too, if the fire she saw burning within their depths now was due to his desire for her . . . or if exhaustion and fear had begun to produce hallucinations of the erotic kind.

She let her gaze slide down his front. He wore a gray wool sport jacket but no tie. His blue cotton shirt was open at the neck, revealing a light dusting of dark hair across his firm, well-muscled chest. Once again she was struck by how he seemed to emanate an aura of unmistakable masculinity, an aura so overpoweringly male, it triggered a responding feminine chord deep within her soul.

A tingling heat swept over her, warming her from her head straight down to her toes.

"I kept hearing Vedder's words playing over and over in my head," she said, knowing that her voice was going a little ragged around the edges—and knowing that it had more to do with the man sitting next to her than with the topic they were discussing.

"I had to try to warn you," she added. "No matter what it took."

He regarded her for a moment. "I . . . I don't know what to say."

She loosened her grip on his forearm. "A thank-you might be nice . . . along with one of those *Maggie darling*s you were tossing my way last night."

He arched an eyebrow at her.

She smiled. "Just to show how much you truly appreciate all my hard work, I mean."

He smiled back, practically dazzling her with his irrepressibly sensuous charm.

"Well, thank you . . . *Maggie darlin'*," he murmured in a voice so downright sexy, it nearly took her breath away.

"You're welcome," she said.

This was crazy, she told herself. She was blushing like some adolescent schoolgirl with her first big crush. True, Jake was a handsome man and, yes, he'd flirted outrageously with her in the piano bar—he'd flirted outrageously enough to melt the bugle beads off her evening gown, as a matter of fact—but he'd also made it abundantly clear that he had no intention of letting their harmless flirtation lead to anything further.

It was a decision she'd told herself she wholeheartedly agreed with. After all, Jake's single-minded obsession with getting his *big story* reminded her too damn much of her father's one-time relentless pursuit of his own career. She knew that after this story broke, there would be another one just as big that Jake would want to pursue, and then another after that. Any relationship with him would have to take a backseat to his career as an investigative journalist, which would never be enough for her.

So why wasn't she backing off now, before the attraction she felt for him got too far out of control?

For that matter, why wasn't he?

"I guess I'm just not used to having people worry about me," he said huskily.

She met his gaze again. A flush had crept into his cheeks, and that smoldering heat in his bluer-than-blue eyes was now burning with enough passion-filled intensity to liquefy titanium.

Her faltering willpower didn't stand a chance, and she had a feeling that neither would his.

"That's too bad," she said. "Because I think it's about time somebody started worrying about you."

She slid her hand over his and gave it a gentle squeeze. The casual contact sent dozens of fiery shivers shimmering down her body.

"I mean, look what you've done in the past twenty-four hours," she said. "Crashing into fundraisers, breaking into hotel rooms, having timber lobbyists plot your murder. I shudder to think what you might get yourself involved with in the next twenty-four, if someone's not there to run interference for you."

He grinned and took her hand, gently rubbing his thumb along her open palm, sending waves of erotic pleasure washing over her.

"Does this mean you're volunteering for the job of watching over me, Ms. Thorpe?" he asked.

Her heart started to pound. Her mouth went dry.

"Well, somebody certainly should," she murmured throatily. "And Lord knows I've never been able to stop myself from tackling those dirty little jobs that no one else seems to want."

"Like kissing tabloid reporters?"

He leaned toward her until his chest brushed lightly against her breasts, until she could feel his pulse racing faster. He leaned in so close that only a heartbeat seemed to separate them.

"Exactly," she murmured, feeling herself flush again. "I guess you could say that those . . . kinds of things . . . hold an irresistible appeal for me."

He slid his hand around her waist, his fingertips burning a path through the flimsy cotton of the football jersey to singe her skin. She shivered.

"Sort of like the way moths are drawn into an open flame," he murmured hoarsely.

His lips brushed lightly over hers. Teasing. Tempting. Tormenting her beyond all endurance.

"Sort of . . . like the way I'm drawn to you," she said in a breathless whisper.

She grasped the lapels of his jacket and pulled him closer until the heat rising off his tightly muscled body felt as if it would simply consume her.

He moaned, then captured her mouth in a fiercely possessive kiss. He forced his tongue between her parted lips, gliding it past her teeth to seek out her tongue, then he stroked it, caressed it with the tip of his own until she moaned softly in response. He slowly raked his fingertips up her back, sending white-hot shivers rippling down her spine. He cupped the back of her head, weaving his fingers through her hair, and pulled her closer to him until only their clothing separated them.

She'd never been kissed this way before, kissed with such passion that it left her weak and utterly defenseless, kissed with such hunger and raw desire that it made her soul tremble from its power.

The movement of his tongue against hers became more erotic still as the kiss grew, deepened. He was kissing her with a calculated slowness, as though he were recording the taste of her in his memory banks for future reference . . . as though she were some forbidden fruit that he was afraid he might never get a chance to taste again. She felt a shudder rack her body.

"Oh, Jake . . ."

She wasn't sure what she was asking him for.

She knew only that she would likely go stark raving mad from unreleased desire if he continued to kiss her this way.

Yet she prayed that he wouldn't stop.

Pulling him closer, she eased her feet out from underneath her and leaned back on the pillows until his arousal pressed hard and strong against her lower abdomen. She slid her hands around his waist, gliding them under his jacket to pull out his shirt and smooth her palms across his fevered skin. Then she arched herself up to meet his hips, urging him closer.

He groaned low in his throat and gently pulled himself away from her.

"This . . . is insane," he said hoarsely.

"Absolutely," she agreed. She reached for him. "Kiss me again."

He shook his head and scrambled off the bed as though the devil himself were trying to seduce him.

"I need—no, *we need*—to get out of here. Now."

He opened the door to his walk-in closet and started sorting through his clothes.

She stared at him, breathless, her body still tingling as if it had been zapped by a few thousand volts of unfiltered electricity.

"Why?" she asked. "Are you afraid Todd will have figured out I'm with you?"

He nodded, then pulled out a pair of blue jeans and a blue and gray flannel shirt.

"But how?" she asked, confused. "I caught a

ride from a truck driver I met at an all-night coffee shop in Studio City. He dropped me off about four blocks from your apartment, right before he got on the freeway to make a five-day run. Nobody knows that I'm here except your landlady, and she thinks I'm your sister."

"Just . . . trust me, okay? We have to leave. And the sooner the better."

"But . . ."

"Please?"

Jake glanced over at her. Passion still burned in the depths of his eyes. It burned with a savagery that made her bones feel as if they would melt from its fierce intensity. But there was something else shining in his eyes just then. The unmistakable look of fear.

A fear that had nothing to do with Todd Mc-Nichols and murder plots.

Jake tossed the clothes onto the bed. "Just get dressed," he said huskily. "We'll go to the paper, try to figure out what we're going to do from there."

Then he turned and left the bedroom without another word of explanation, just as he'd done in the piano bar the night before. Only this time Maggie understood why he'd left so abruptly. Jake was afraid, nearly terrified out of his wits, by the power of what he felt for her.

Maggie sank back onto the bed and smiled.

Oddly enough, it was the best news she'd heard all day.

FIVE

"Judas H. Priest!"

Jake leaned against the kitchen counter and closed his eyes, taking a series of slow, deep breaths. His body felt as tightly strung as an old rubber band that was stretched past its breaking point and would likely snap given the smallest of provocations.

This had to be how the descent into sheer lunacy starts, he decided, raking his still-tingling fingers through his hair, when the irrational seems not only totally logical but desirable as well. He knew he should just stay the hell away from Maggie Thorpe—keeping a continent between them might do for starters—but he couldn't seem to help himself no matter how hard he tried.

It was as though he couldn't think straight when she was in the same room with him, gazing up at him with those wickedly sexy hazel eyes of hers, plying him with her soul-incinerating smiles and softly feminine charms until the last of his resolutions to keep his emotional distance from her completely faded away.

It was as though he couldn't think of anything at all except how good it would feel to kiss her, of how mind-blowingly, unbelievably satisfying it would be to feel her mouth open to the demanding thrust of his tongue . . . and to feel her own tongue returning his kisses with wild, wanton abandon.

Or how inconceivably pleasurable it would feel to weave his fingers through her long, silky golden-blond hair and pull her closer to him . . . having her every curve pressed intimately against his . . . feeling her heart pound with the same erratic rhythm of his . . . feeling her body heat rise over him in a fiery rush that would scorch his very soul.

He drew another deep breath. Hell, his fantasies about Maggie were bad enough. Knowing that following through on his desires could feel far better than anything his overactive imagination might ever come up with was even worse.

Because, truth told, that kiss back in McNichols's hotel suite had sealed Jake's fate long before he'd given in to the impulse to kiss her again moments earlier.

He wanted her even though he knew that prolonged exposure to those erotic kisses and intoxicating caresses of hers would likely send his soul into anaphylactic shock.

Muttering another curse, he opened his eyes and made a grab for the telephone receiver on the wall.

This is ridiculous, Jake thought. Maggie was in danger—real danger—and he was allowing his hormones to cloud his common sense. His first priority should be to ensure her safety, to provide her with a sanctuary where she could wait out the crisis—a place preferably as far away from him as possible.

Maggie was right about not going to the police. They couldn't, at least not yet. Which left them with only one choice as far as Jake could see—namely, for him to break the story of the senator's involvement with Vedder within the pages of the *Sentinel* . . . and throw in a few highly incriminating details about what Maggie had overheard in the senator's suite while he was at it too.

But breaking the story would take time. Thus far, all Jake had were numerous photographs of McNichols and his trusty campaign manager Raymond Kingfisher meeting with Karl Vedder in San Francisco. Without the packet of receipts from Jake's informant to back up the accusations of senatorial improprieties, the article was a no-go. *That* was one lesson Jake had learned the hard way. Too bad he hadn't learned the same lesson about staying away from heiresses.

Scowling, he punched in the number for his editor, Louis Ashkenazi, only to get a busy signal. Jake terminated the call, then pressed the code for automatic redial once the line was free, and slipped the receiver back onto its hook on the wall.

"Private Thorpe reporting as ordered . . . sir."

Maggie's softly feminine voice came from the edge of the hallway. He glanced in her direction.

She gave him a little salute, then extended her hands out from her sides, as though she were awaiting his inspection.

He let his gaze slide over her. She'd pulled her hair back into a ponytail and put on the clothes that he'd laid out for her, although they seemed a good two sizes too big for her slender build. To compensate, she'd tucked in the plaid cotton shirt and tightened the loose waistband of the jeans with a thin black leather belt. Then she'd rolled up the wrist-length sleeves to her elbows and flipped up the shirt's collar to frame her face.

For having gotten dressed in something under ten minutes—and for only having gotten an hour's sleep at most—Maggie looked casually elegant. And far too sexy for his own peace of mind.

His body started to tighten, grow hard all over again. He drew a deep, steadying breath and held it a moment, trying to refocus.

"That's . . . fine," he said. "But you're going to need to wear a hat before we go out. Something with a wide brim to hide your face."

She put her hands on her hips. "I don't look that bad, do I?"

Then she gave him a smile so warmly erotic, it could endanger the integrity of the polar ice caps.

Liquefied heat started to race through his veins again, firing his already-overheated libido into an immediate overdrive.

"No, you look . . . fine," he mumbled, feeling himself start to flush. "I just don't want to run the risk of your being recognized, that's all."

She stared at him for a moment longer, then slowly nodded.

"I, ah, hope you don't mind," she said, moving into the kitchen to stand next to him. "I had to punch another hole in your belt before I could wear it."

"No . . . problem," he murmured huskily.

A ruined belt was the least of his concerns, even if it was his favorite.

Her smile only grew wider. It was as if she knew full well the devastating effect she had upon both his libido and his heart, and it pleased her to no end.

She lightly skimmed her fingertips down his arm in a touch so soft, he could scarcely feel it through the lightweight wool of his jacket, yet it burned his skin all the same. He tried to suppress a shudder, but couldn't.

"I'm afraid it'll probably never be the same," she said. "Your belt, I mean."

The telephone started to ring, signaling that Ashkenazi's line was free.

Jake stared into her laughing hazel eyes for a moment before reaching for the receiver.

Hell, he could probably say the same thing about his emotional defense system. A few more hours spent with Maggie Thorpe, and it'd never be the same again either.

They made the drive over to the *Sentinel* in under ten minutes, mostly because Jake shattered every speed limit and ignored every stop sign they encountered along the way. If Maggie had been prone to bouts of paranoia, she might have thought his haste to get to his office was due less to his desire to take action against Todd than it was because he couldn't bear to spend another second alone with her than was absolutely necessary. Jake had dumped her in the newsroom's glass-enclosed conference room the moment they had arrived and had gone off to wait—none too patiently—in front of his editor's private office for Louis Ashkenazi to join them, rather than stay with her.

Sighing, Maggie settled back in an uncomfortable straight-backed chair and peered through a crack in the blinds to regard the object of her thoughts—and her biggest source of irritation at the moment.

Jake was pacing back and forth in front of Ashkenazi's office like a caged jungle cat, his hands shoved into the pockets of his gunmetal-gray trousers, his muscled body visibly rigid with tension. A shock of his tousled black hair fell rakishly across his brow, giving him a bad-boy charm that she found irresistibly appealing. Even with the threatening scowl etched across his handsome face, she still thought he was the sexiest man she'd ever laid eyes on. Not to mention one of the most difficult men she'd ever tried to figure out.

She frowned and dropped the blinds.

What was it with this guy anyway? One minute he was sending her pulses racing with the stroke of his hand against her cheek . . . or firing her imagination into near erotic meltdown with a deep voice that was as sexy as sin . . . or overwhelming her emotions with a kiss that positively curled her toes and left her breathless and weak as a little lamb. And the next minute . . .

Well, the next, he was acting as though he wasn't interested in anything she had to offer—or worse, that he'd built a stone wall around his heart that was as unlikely of being breached as the legendary walls of Jericho.

More important than *his* inexplicable emotional flipflops, what was it with *her*?

After all, she knew there was no way that things could ever work out between them. He'd made that clear enough. Getting his story was more important to him than anything else, and the worst part was she couldn't really blame him for feeling that way.

She had known Jake's name was vaguely familiar when she'd met him, but it had taken David Mayron's comment at the fund-raiser to jog her memory. There had been some kind of scandal four years before, something about a story that Jake had broken which had been proven false. Although she didn't remember all the details, she knew Jake had lost his job, which was probably why he was now working for what was little more than a glorified tabloid. The right story, though, could put him back on the top.

This story.

The door to the conference room swung open. Maggie glanced up. Jake and a wiry-looking older man with unkempt curly dark brown hair and silver-rimmed glasses entered the room.

Jake met her gaze long enough for her to see the hunger, the all-consuming need still burning in his bluer-than-blue eyes, then he looked away.

Knowing how he felt about his career—and how he said he *didn't* feel about her—ought to be enough to convince her to leave him alone for both their sakes, and yet . . . she couldn't just walk away.

How could she walk away when she felt more attracted, more connected to Jake than she'd been to any man in a long, long time? How could she do it when she knew in her heart that he felt the same way about her even if he was too damned stubborn to admit it?

"Maggie, this is my editor, Louis Ashkenazi," Jake said quietly, closing the door behind him. "Lou, meet Maggie Thorpe."

"Well, I'll be damned," Ashkenazi murmured,

walking toward the table. His face was nearly split in two by the size of his smile. "You weren't lying, Jake. It really *is* her."

His enthusiasm was so genuine, Maggie couldn't help but smile back.

"In the proverbial flesh," she said.

She removed the well-worn cowboy hat that Jake had slapped on her head before they'd left his apartment some thirty minutes earlier and slid it onto the table. He'd insisted she keep its brim pulled low across her forehead to prevent anyone from recognizing her, although, thus far, she thought he was worrying over nothing. She'd already walked past Liebowitz and Brenner—two men who'd shadowed her every move two summers before—and they hadn't so much as even glanced in her direction.

She extended her hand across the table. "It's nice to meet you, Lou."

"Same here."

He shook her hand then slowly released it, his smile growing wider.

"Maggie Thorpe," he said, repeating her name as though he couldn't quite believe his good fortune. He sank down onto the chair closest to him, then glanced back at Jake, who was slowly making his way toward them.

"Do you have any idea what this means, Jake?" Ashkenazi asked.

Jake shrugged and took the seat directly across from Maggie.

"Why, it's damn near the exclusive of the decade," Ashkenazi went on, his voice swelling with pride. "America's favorite deb's on the run, and the *Sentinel* is the one place she turns for help. Jake, I swear, I'm so happy right now, I could kiss you."

Maggie grinned. "Oh, I wouldn't recommend doing anything as rash as all that."

"No?" Ashkenazi glanced back at her, still smiling. "And why's that?"

Maggie's gaze shot toward Jake. His expression was closed, unreadable.

"Personal experience," she said, unable to resist teasing Jake a little. "When Raymond Kingfisher nearly caught Jake snooping through Todd's suite last night, I suggested Jake kiss me to throw Raymond off. From the fuss Jake made about it, you'd have thought I'd suggested he loan me a kidney or something."

A few seconds passed, then the trace of a smile began to hover around Jake's lips.

"You'd have done better asking me for the kidney," he murmured. "I'd have given you *that* gladly."

Ashkenazi chuckled softly.

"But not a kiss?" she asked, keeping her gaze locked with Jake's. "You wouldn't give me one teensy little kiss . . . even when it could have saved your hide?"

"*Cost* me my hide is more like it, Maggie darlin'," he said. "Kingfisher looked like he wanted to have me stuffed and mounted right there on the spot."

His Georgia drawl was low and soft and unrelentingly sensual. The sound of it sent dozens of electrically charged quivers surging through her, making her body tingle all over and her breath go all ragged and frayed around the edges.

Then he smiled at her, which seemed to magnify the shiver-inducing effects of those electrically charged quivers about two hundred percent.

"Kissing you can be downright dangerous," he said.

But not nearly as dangerous as your smile can be, she thought, feeling her heart skip a beat.

Her own smile grew wider. Not breaking eye contact, she propped her elbows on the table and leaned forward, resting her chin on her open palms.

"But I thought all you hotshot reporters thrived on danger," she said. "You know, cloaks and daggers? Feats of derring-do? Remember Woodward and Bernstein? And then there's that guy from Desert Storm who kept broadcasting with missiles firing all around him. Didn't they call him the scud stud or something?"

Jake gave her an all-out grin this time, complete with winking dimple. "Yeah, but there are just some things too dangerous for a reporter to attempt even for the sake of a big story."

She arched her eyebrows. "And kissing *me* is one of them, I suppose?"

"Oh, absolutely. It's even listed on page one of

our survival manual as things to avoid at all costs . . . remind me to show you a copy of it sometime."

Ashkenazi laughed loud and long and heartily enough to bring her crashing back to reality. For a moment she'd almost forgotten that the newspaper editor was there in the room with them. For a moment the whole world had seemed to consist of only her and Jake.

"Sounds to me like you two had quite a night last night," Ashkenazi said, folding his arms against his chest to eye them both with a newspaperman's ingrained curiosity. "So what happened when Kingfisher came into the room and caught you kissing . . . or dare I even ask?"

Jake leaned back in his chair, suddenly looking as uncomfortable as she felt herself. He cleared his throat. "Ah, nothing much," he murmured. "Kingfisher just kicked us out of the room. Things got interesting about an hour or so later though."

Jake glanced back at her. "Maggie, why don't you tell Lou what you overheard Kingfisher and Vedder discussing when you returned to your room."

She nodded. "Okay."

Then she took a deep breath—more to restore the breath she'd lost from staring so intently into Jake's eyes than from anything else—and filled Ashkenazi in on what she'd overheard.

"You've done a helluva lot more than step on a few toes this time," Ashkenazi muttered once she'd finished. "And I get the funniest feeling that our friend Vedder isn't going to be satisfied with tossing a brickbat through your car windshield like those strike organizers did last June over in Compton."

Jake shrugged. "I'm a big boy, Lou. I can take care of myself. Besides, Maggie's the one I'm worried about here. She can't go to the police without any evidence to back up her allegations, and until my article is published, she's a walking target for McNichols's henchmen."

"But that's just plain silly," Maggie said, frowning. "Todd wouldn't dare try to harm me no matter what I may have overheard. He just wouldn't."

Jake's gaze met hers again. "I wish I could be as confident about that as you are. Because I suspect they're now planning an *accident* for two."

"I agree with Jake, Maggie," Ashkenazi said, looking worried. "I got a call a little while ago from one of the paper's informants. He thought I'd be interested in hearing the latest scuttlebutt about your disappearance. McNichols's people have put the word out. They're offering a substantial reward for your recovery and return to campaign headquarters . . . and no questions asked about how anyone may have accomplished it either."

A chill slid down her spine.

"So how do you want to handle the situation?" Ashkenazi asked, turning to Jake. "Put Maggie under wraps for a while?"

Jake nodded. "Keep her someplace safe until

the story breaks. Someplace where she won't run the risk of being recognized—which may have to be the North Pole considering her high profile."

"About how long are you figuring it'll take for the story?"

"Five days. A week at the most. My source at Vedder's D.C. office has promised to send me copies of receipts for some all-expense-paid Caribbean excursions the senator took courtesy of Vedder and the timber industry. He's being watched, so he has to be careful. But those receipts, coupled with the photos I already have of Vedder meeting privately with both McNichols and Kingfisher, ought to be enough to go forward with the original article. As for Maggie's involvement, I can layer in that part in about twenty minutes on the computer."

"Sounds reasonable," Ashkenazi said.

Then he was silent for a moment or two, as though he were mulling over the problem in his mind.

"As for where to stash her," Ashkenazi said, "I've got an idea, although it's not as remote as the North Pole. My cabin in the San Bernardino Mountains is small—only one room with a partitioned-off kitchen—but I think it'd be the perfect place for you two to hide out until this thing is over."

"*You two?*" Jake repeated. "Now, wait a minute, Lou. I'm not going anywhere."

Ashkenazi turned toward Maggie. "I'd better warn you," he said, ignoring Jake's protests. "It's pretty rustic. I use it when I want to get away from it all, do some fishing, reading with no outside distractions. The wife hates it. There's limited electricity from a generator in the back, although a good stiff breeze will usually conk it out. No phone, of course, but Jake could take his cellular. And, ah, no indoor plumbing," he added sheepishly, "although the water pump in the kitchen works okay if you prime it for a while first."

"No indoor plumbing?" Maggie asked, not sure if she had heard him correctly or not. "Then how are we supposed to . . . ?"

Ashkenazi grinned. "There's an outhouse about ten feet from the back door," he said. "Like I said, it's pretty rustic. The cabin's out in the middle of nowhere, not another soul around for miles. You and Jake may get bored with all the back-to-nature stuff, but at least you'll both be out of harm's way."

"I told you I'm not going," Jake said again, more forcefully this time. "I've never run from a story in my life, and I'm not about to start now."

"And I'd rather lose you to a rival paper than to one of those *accidents* Vedder was talking about arranging for you," Ashkenazi shot back. "Besides, we can't just leave Maggie out there all by herself, and the fewer people we bring in on this the better. Hell, the cabin is bare-bones basics, man. She'll need some help with the generator at the very least. And having you out of McNichols's sight will make me sleep a lot easier."

"But—"

"No buts. You're going with her," Ashkenazi said. "End of discussion."

"But what if Maggie doesn't want to go to the mountains?" Jake asked, clutching at the proverbial straws. "Maybe she'd prefer someplace not so back-to-nature. Maybe she'd be more comfortable staying at some out-of-state resort under an assumed name."

"Oh, don't be silly, Jake," she murmured, reaching for the hat. "I think Lou's cabin is a wonderful idea, especially since we don't seem to have any other options. Besides, I've always enjoyed camping out. It should be fun."

She slipped the cowboy hat back on her head, pulled its rim low over her forehead, and flashed Jake her brightest smile.

"When do we leave?"

Jake was still grumbling about the cabin when they left the *Sentinel*'s newsroom an hour later.

"It's not too late to change your mind," he said, unlocking the passenger door of his Honda Accord. His forehead was etched in a frown, and he looked as nervous and jumpy as a beleaguered fox on the run for his life from a pack of hounds.

"We don't have to do this," he said. "We can find another solution."

"I know, darling," she said, reaching for the door handle. "I know."

Her arm brushed against his chest long enough

for her to feel his body heat seeping through the cotton fabric of his shirt . . . and for her own body to shiver in response.

Jake jerked away from her as though he'd been burned. "There *has* to be another solution," he muttered. "There just has to be."

"But the cabin is the only practical option we have available to us right now," she argued. "It's isolated, so there won't be any other people around, which is what you said was the most important thing. That we stay out of sight."

"I said *you* should stay out of sight. I never said I had to."

She gave him a smile. "Besides," she went on, "I'm kind of looking forward to it. Who knows? Staying at Lou's cabin could turn out to be some great romantic adventure."

"A romantic adventure?" He practically sputtered the words. "Is that what you think this is?"

She slid into the car seat. "I said it had the potential for becoming one," she corrected him softly. "Provided, of course, we both relaxed and tried to have some fun."

He mumbled something she couldn't quite hear, then closed her car door with more force than was absolutely necessary. He circled the Honda and got in on the driver's side.

"I think we'd better set some ground rules before we go any further with this," he said.

She grinned. "What kind did you have in mind?

Like who cooks and who does the cleanup afterward? I vote we simply take turns."

Either task would likely be difficult. The stove was supposedly a woodburning antique, and the water had to be pumped by hand at the kitchen sink and then heated in a large pot over the stove before they could wash the dishes.

He shook his head, jabbing his car key into the ignition. "Those aren't the kind of ground rules I was referring to."

"Then what kind *did* you mean?"

He drew a deep breath, held it for a moment, then exhaled. He turned to look at her, keeping his hand resting on the ignition.

"The cabin has one room, Maggie," he said quietly. "And only one bed. Lou says there's an oversize easy chair in the corner, but still the sleeping arrangements will be . . . well, problematic."

Poor darling, she thought with a smile. He really was working himself into a fine state of panic over this.

"I don't want to give you the wrong impression about what will be happening at the cabin once we get there," he went on. "Between us, I mean." He regarded her solemnly for a moment. "I don't want you to be thinking that we'll simply pick up where we left off this morning back in my bedroom . . . because we won't."

Maggie felt something tighten deep inside her, as though a fist were squeezing a bit of the life right out of her soul. She leaned forward until they were only inches away from each other.

"But why not?" she asked. "After all, we're both well over the age of consent, and you *are* single, aren't you, Jake?"

He nodded. "I've been divorced for almost four years. And before you ask, no, I'm not seeing anyone special right now. Getting my career back on track has taken most of my free time and energy."

She drew a sigh of relief. "Good. You already know that I'm not involved with anyone."

"Yes, but—"

"And you certainly didn't hear me registering any complaints about our kiss this morning, now, did you?" she went on, ignoring him. She leaned a little closer. "As a matter of fact, if you should feel the urge to kiss me again—say, right now, for example—why, I assure you I wouldn't mind it in the least."

She held his gaze for a moment, watching the play of emotions flash across his face. Hunger. Need. Desire. Fear. They all seemed to be wrapped up in the same enigmatic package.

He lifted his hand as though he were going to stroke her cheek. Instead, he gently grasped her shoulder and pushed her back onto her side of the car.

"It's . . . not . . . that I don't find you attractive," he said huskily. "Because I do." He drew a slow deep breath. "Probably too damn much, in fact."

"That's good, because I feel the same way about you," she said, reaching for him.

"But it'd never work out," he said, stopping her. "For starters, I don't handle flings with heiresses all that well, and getting involved would be too damned complicated. That's why I think the best thing for us to do would be to get our hormones under control before we end up doing anything that we'll only regret later."

"Oh? And just how do you propose we control our hormones?" she teased. "String an old blanket from the ceiling to separate us at night? Stay at least five feet away from each other in the day?"

"If we have to," he said. His gaze didn't waver. "Because I'm serious about this, Maggie. I'm not right for you . . . and you're not right for me. Pretending otherwise could only hurt us both."

She regarded him quietly for a moment, wishing that she could tell him that he was wrong, wishing that she could tell him how perfect they were for each other, even though logic told her that he was right.

But how were they supposed to keep their hormones under control when they were going to be spending the next week together in a one-room cabin with nothing but time on their hands to gaze longingly into each other's eyes . . . and to fantasize about doing a lot more than that?

Maggie took a slow, deep breath.

Hell, if you asked her, it was going to take a lot more than sheer willpower to keep them apart, and a lot more than Jake's own version of the walls of Jericho, which seemed to her to be crumbling by the moment.

Although she saw no reason to point out either of those facts to him.

After all, there were just some things a man had to find out for himself.

SIX

"Why are you being so unreasonable?" Maggie asked, holding a pair of royal blue silk pajamas up to her chest. "You know I wouldn't ask if I didn't think we needed them. Now, surely we can squeeze enough pennies out of the budget so we could get at least one pair?"

She was smiling at him as she made her pitch— it was her warmest and most inviting smile yet, Jake decided—and her voice was so alluringly feminine that he figured it wouldn't take much more persuasion on her part for him to surrender his entire wallet . . . if not a rather large piece of his heart.

"Please?" she asked.

"Well . . ."

He took a deep breath and shook his head.

"No," he said. "Put them back. Hell, we're almost tapped out as it is without indulging in unnecessary luxuries."

"Luxuries? Trust me, darling, considering where we're going, a pair of pajamas will be more like an absolute necessity."

"No."

He gave his already-filled-to-overflowing shopping cart a gentle shove and started slowly pushing it down the narrow aisle of the Real McCoy's Country Store toward the checkout stand.

They were in Cedar's Glen, a small community just outside of Lake Arrowhead and about an hour's drive from the cabin. They were purchasing the personal items they'd need for their week-long stay up in the San Bernardino Mountains.

Because Maggie had left all her belongings back at the hotel—and because Lou thought it would be running too much of a risk for Jake to return to his apartment for his own things—the *Sentinel* had authorized an expense account of close to two thousand dollars, the most the paper had ever allotted Jake for an assignment.

They'd already used about a third of that to rent a Jeep Wrangler for the trek up to the cabin, and Maggie, it seemed, was doing her damnedest to spend whatever remained in the overpriced store before they ever reached the supermarket to stock up on food.

"But couldn't we get just one pair?" she asked, falling into step beside him, still clutching those damned pajamas to her chest.

"No. How many times do I have to remind you

that we're on a strict budget? We can't afford to buy everything that catches your fancy."

Especially when he could well imagine just how sexy she'd look in silk pajamas, even oversize ones. That was one temptation he didn't think he'd need up at the cabin.

"But . . . oh, you're just being ridiculous!" she said. "We're talking only fifty lousy dollars. That's hardly going to break us."

She made a grab for the shopping cart, slowing it to a stop.

"Besides, I want pajamas," she said, meeting his gaze. "We can put back a pair of jeans if we have to, or one of the shirts, whatever it takes."

Jake glanced toward the front of the store. The proprietors—an older couple in their late sixties who, according to the framed photograph above the front door, were Vic and Libby McCoy—were checking out another customer, although it seemed to Jake that their attention was more focused on what Jake and Maggie were arguing about than anything else.

For the past fifteen minutes or so, Jake could have sworn that the older couple had been staring at them, following their every move through the store with an intense personal interest that bordered on scrutiny.

Damn, Jake thought.

Piquing anyone's curiosity was the last thing they needed, since Maggie's face, even shaded by the cowboy hat, was more recognizable than the president's, thanks to the local news stations' hourly updates on her disappearance.

As though she'd felt his sudden apprehension, Maggie glanced over her shoulder at the checkout stand.

"What I mean," Maggie went on, lowering her voice as she turned back to face him, "is that we can't very well sleep in our clothes for the next five days. We'll need some pajamas. At least one pair that we could share."

He frowned. "You want to share them?" he asked, keeping his own voice just as low as hers had been. "How? I wear them one night and you the next?"

She smiled. "Actually, I was thinking more that I could wear the top and you the bottom."

The lights in her hazel eyes started to twinkle at the prospect of creating more mischief. Then her smile grew absolutely naughty.

"Although your plan does sound much more intriguing than mine," she murmured. "Taking turns sleeping in the buff, I mean."

Jake drew a deep breath, held it for a moment, then slowly exhaled.

The thought of Maggie fully undressed aroused him to the point of near pain. Thinking about her blond hair cascading around her smooth, tanned shoulders in silken, honey-colored waves that his fingers itched to wind their way through . . .

Thinking about her full, rounded breasts being finally freed from oversize football jerseys, chambray shirts, and lacy brassieres, ready to fill the palms of his hands . . . of their rose-colored nipples ready to be molded into tightened buds by his thumb and forefinger . . .

Or of her narrow waist and generously curved hips, so perfectly proportioned, and how his lips would nibble a path along them until she arched her slender body toward his mouth, burning from his touch, begging for more than just his kisses . . .

And of her legs. Legs so long they seemed to stretch halfway to Georgia. Tanned, strong legs that he knew she'd wrap tightly around his hips when they made love, hugging him close to her until she shattered his control, conquered his soul.

He drew another breath, sharper this time, as he felt his body grow tighter still. His mouth went dry. His abdominal muscles began to constrict.

"Speaking strictly for myself, of course," Maggie went on, letting her gaze slide slowly down his body, arousing him even further with her too-frank appraisal. "I, ah, doubt if your plan would work. Because knowing that you were in the buff, lying only a few tantalizing feet away from me . . ."

She met his gaze. She looked as flushed as he felt himself.

"Well, let's just say that it will take a lot more than an old blanket strung across the room to keep my hormones in line," she added huskily.

His, too, for that matter.

"Okay," he murmured hoarsely. "Fine. We'll get some pajamas."

He reached toward the shelf next to them and pulled out a cellophane-wrapped pair of black and red checked flannel pajamas.

"But cotton, not silk," he said. "Okay?"

She grinned and tossed the royal blue pajamas back onto the shelf.

"Cotton would be just fine, darling," she said. "And thank you."

Jake nodded, then pushed the cart down the aisle and over to the counter just as the last customer was leaving the store.

Vic McCoy gave them both a toothy grin. "Howdy, folks. Welcome to Real McCoy's. I'm Vic and this here's my wife, Libby."

"How do," Libby murmured politely, although she was eyeing Maggie with a bit more interest and curiosity than suited Jake's comfort level.

Maggie flashed a smile. "Hello. I'm Ellen," she said glibly. "And this is my husband, Peter Warren."

They'd agreed on the need for aliases when they rented the Jeep. Since Peter Warren was the name Jake always used when he worked undercover on a story—out of homage to his favorite cinematic reporter played to jaded perfection by Clark Gable in *It Happened One Night*—he'd suggested he use the same name. Maggie, with her eyes twinkling like mad, had told him that she thought it a great choice. Then she'd coyly selected Ellen as her alias,

which was the name of Claudette Colbert's charac-
ter—and Gable's love interest—from the same film.

Vic nodded. "You folks just passing through, or
are you planning to stay in Cedar's Glen for a
while?" he asked, punching in the code for the flannel pajamas on the cash register.

"Ah, just passing through mainly," Jake said,
spinning his own part of the yarn. "We got a deal
on a condo over in Arrowhead for the next week.
We live down in Bakersfield, thought we'd take a
few days off and enjoy the lake before it got too
cold."

Libby snagged her husband's shirt-sleeve. "Pa, I
tell you, it's her," she whispered.

She pushed a folded newspaper at her husband
and tapped at the front page, which had a glamour
shot of Maggie plastered across it.

"She's that missing heiress everybody's been
talking about," Libby added.

Jake started to tense. He glanced at Maggie,
afraid to move, afraid to even breathe.

"Wait a minute. A *boom box*?"

Maggie's voice rang out loud and angry enough
to make the canned goods in the cart start to rattle
together.

Vic and Libby flinched as though they'd been
slapped. They lowered the paper.

Maggie reached into the cart and grabbed the
portable radio/CD player by its black plastic handle.

"Dammit, Peter, what is this doing in here? You

keep harping on me about our budget and all, and yet here you are, getting this thing, when we'd hadn't so much as discussed it!"

Jake exhaled. "What the hell was there to discuss?" he asked, following her lead. "I liked it, so I got it. Big deal."

"Oh, really?"

She set the boom box down on the counter with a tad more force than was necessary.

"So it's okay for you to buy another stupid toy, but I can't have one measly pair of silk pajamas? Just like it's okay for you to sit around the house all day drinking beer while I'm busting my chops pulling double shifts down at the Crow's Nest? Is that it?"

"Dammit, Ellen, would you just lay off me? You know the doctor says I can't work because of my bad back."

Vic and Libby exchanged a quick glance, as though they wished they were anyplace else than at ground zero of what promised to be a highly volatile marital explosion.

"That was two years ago, Peter," Maggie snapped. "If you ask me, your back seems fine now."

"Well, excuse me. I didn't realize you were trained to dispense medical advice along with cocktails."

"Very funny."

Maggie folded her arms over her chest and glared at him.

"You know, my mother was right about you all along," she said. "Sometimes I don't know why I even bother to stick around!"

"Oh, yeah?" Jake's voice rose an octave or two. "Well, who needs you? It'd suit me just fine, wifey dear, if you packed up your stuff and went back home to live with your mother."

"Well, maybe I will! It's not like you'd *care* if I did anyway!"

The last words came out with a broken sob. Then Maggie covered her face with her hands as though she were suddenly racked with tears and ran out of the store.

"Aw, quit your bawling!" Jake yelled after her.

Remembering to scowl—although he felt more like grinning—Jake turned back to face Vic and Libby.

"Look, I ain't got all day," Jake added in a growl. "Are you gonna ring up our order or not?"

Vic glanced at Libby, who murmured something that sounded a lot like "What must I have been thinking?" and dropped the folded newspaper into the trash can behind the counter.

"Sure, Peter," Vic said, reaching for another item from the cart. "Right away."

Libby gave Jake a motherly smile, the kind that offered oodles of sympathy over a doomed marriage with nary a suggestion that his cocktail-waitress wife might be the missing heiress that all of America would likely be searching for come nightfall.

"Honey, which would you prefer?" she asked. "Paper or plastic?"

Maggie nervously paced around the parking lot of the Real McCoy's Country Store, wondering what could possibly be taking Jake so long and if her alter ego, Ellen, should storm back in to get him, spouting even more faked tears and hurled accusations of marital discord.

She was about to mount the rescue attempt when the door opened and he walked out, pushing a paper-bag-filled shopping cart.

"Well?" she asked, hurrying over to join him at the back of the Jeep. "Did they buy it?"

He grinned. "Like a pair of greedy real estate developers snapping up a plot of prime Florida swampland. I may be overly optimistic here, Maggie darlin', but I think our new friend Libby may even want to set us up with some marriage counseling."

He reached past the spare tire, which was mounted on the back of the Jeep, and opened the rear door, then began transferring the bags from the cart to the Jeep.

"Well, that's a relief," Maggie said, leaning against the sun-warmed Jeep, feeling suddenly exhausted. She stifled a yawn. "Because for a while there, I had my doubts we could pull it off."

"Well, I didn't," he said. "You made a great save. In fact, you were pretty damned impressive."

Maggie grinned back at him, not feeling quite so tired now, and picked up one of the bags.

"Why, thank you," she said. "It's nice to know those summer extension courses I took in theater weren't a total waste of Father's money after all."

She set the bag into the trunk, then turned back to the cart.

"Besides, you weren't so bad back there yourself . . . *Peter*," she teased.

"Yeah, well, it's that reporter's survival manual I was telling you about. It has a whole section devoted to delicate operations just like these." Then his grin deepened. "With the two of us working together, Vic and Libby didn't stand a chance."

She laughed and reached for the last bag at the same time he did. Fingertips grazed fingertips, producing enough sparks at the brief contact to cause spontaneous combustion. She drew a sharp breath as a rush of sensual heat washed over her, warming her from the inside out until her whole body began to tingle.

She glanced up at him, feeling her pulse begin to race, her heart start to flutter.

"I'm glad you're finally beginning to catch on, Mr. Wilder," she said huskily, keeping her gaze locked with his. "That we make a perfect couple, I mean."

She could see the war of emotions flash across his handsome face. He swallowed hard. "Yeah, I guess we do . . . when all we're doing is pretending."

His voice sounded as shadowed as her own had been, although a tad rougher around its edges perhaps.

Then he took a deep breath. "Too bad we both have to live in the real world, Maggie."

He grabbed the last bag and shoved it into the trunk, slamming the door closed afterward.

"Look, it's, ah, getting late," he said, avoiding looking straight at her. "We'd better get to the market for some food and head up to the cabin before nightfall."

Then, without waiting to hear her reply, he pushed the cart away and walked around the Jeep to the driver's side, running away from her again . . . running away from his feelings, the way he always did.

The worst part was that all she could do was stand there and watch him go.

After their quick run by the supermarket for food—and the bumpier than expected drive up the mountain—they arrived at the cabin at a few minutes after five.

Jake killed the engine and immediately got out to unload their supplies, but Maggie sat in the Jeep for a moment longer, staring at their temporary home.

The roughhewn log cabin was small, probably not even as large as her parents' bedroom back on their San Francisco estate, but she still thought it utterly charming. With the insight of a true romantic, Lou had built the cabin in the middle of a natural clearing, so close to the edge of the dense pine forest that Maggie could well imagine deer wandering into the front yard in the early mornings and raccoons foraging for food in the back late at night.

"You coming in?" Jake asked, walking past the Jeep with his arms full of supplies. "Or have you changed your mind already?"

She laughed. "Not a chance."

She opened the door of the Jeep and got out. She took a deep breath, filling her lungs to their limit with the crisp, clean scent of the mountain, of tangy pine needles and a hint of sweet sage. A slight chill hugged the September air, although fall was a few weeks away and winter further still. At the edge of the clearing, tall, spindly pines shot straight up into a seemingly endless blue sky, and the only sounds to break the mountain's silence were the chirping of birds and the whisper of wind through the pine needles.

After a lifetime spent living in the grime, smog, and constant noise of the city, Maggie decided that this could very well be heaven—a heaven that she and Jake had all to themselves for the next week.

Smiling, she grabbed a couple of bags of groceries from the back of the Jeep and walked toward the cabin just as Jake was leaving to pick up another load.

He cocked an eyebrow at her, although he didn't slow down.

"You sure you don't want to turn around and head back to civilization?" he teased. "Maybe book a suite at the Bel-Air or something?"

"Don't be silly," she said. "I think it's beautiful. In fact, I may never want to leave."

She stepped inside the cabin and slowed to a stop, glancing from the lumpy-looking easy chair, scuffed oak end table, and battered metal floor lamp in one corner, over to the even lumpier-looking double bed shoved against a wall in the next. The whitewashed walls were bare, and the ceiling was a series of crisscrossed natural wood beams. A mostly threadbare navy blue and white braided rug lay across the unpolished hardwood floor.

She moved her gaze on to the spartanlike kitchen at the opposite end of the room. It had a small refrigerator, an antique metal sink complete with hand pump, a woodburning stove, and a back-door access to the infamous outhouse. It offered the basic necessities and nothing more.

Still, she liked it. The cabin had a cozy, homey feel. It struck her as being the kind of a place where a person could curl up in a chair and read for hours without interruption, since its only source of potential distraction appeared to be a large window next to the bed . . . and an unobstructed view of the mountain that took her breath away nearly as much as Jake did.

She moved into the kitchen and dropped the bag of groceries onto the butcher-block table.

"Of course you say you love it now," Jake said, walking back into the cabin with two more paper bags tucked under his arms.

His voice was still as light and teasing as before, although Maggie detected a serious undertone that hadn't been there earlier.

"But just wait until you want to take a bath and realize you'll have to sponge off with heated water at the stove," he said. "Or when the electricity fails, and we can't get the generator running again—provided, of course, that we can even get it running now. Lou hasn't been out here for at least six months."

She sighed. "I wish you'd stop treating me like some hothouse flower who can't survive for ten minutes in the real world. I'm going to be fine, Jake. Honest."

She reached for one of the bags in his arms, moving close enough for the masculine scent of his cologne to swirl around her and send her pulse racing out of control. She drew a deep breath, moved back an inch or two, and set the bag on the table.

"Besides," she went on, "we're always having problems with the emergency generator out at Pet Haven. It takes the electricians at least twenty-four hours to respond to our call, so I've gotten pretty good at repairing the damn thing myself. Once we've finished unpacking, I'll go out and take a look at this one."

Jake started to smile.

"The 'deb of the decade' rolling up her sleeves to work on a generator?"

He slid his bag onto the table next to hers.

"Aren't you afraid the governing committee will strip you of your title when they find out?" he asked.

"I should only be so lucky," she said with a laugh, heading toward the front door to bring in more supplies. "Believe me, being thought of as some pampered little debutante is not my idea of a good time."

Especially when she was convinced she was falling in love with the man who thought it was. He'd made his low disregard for all debs more than abundantly clear.

"Even without the fun of being hounded by a pack of tabloid reporters all the time," she added.

She tossed the last words over her shoulder once she reached the Jeep. She grabbed two of the bags that contained the clothes they'd picked up at the Real McCoy's along with the boom box.

"Why, when it's a slow news day," she said, turning back around to face him, "they follow me all over town, hoping against hope that I'll do something even remotely scandalous that they can write about. When I don't, they either rehash the past or just make up something new."

He gave her an all-out grin this time, complete with winking dimple. She felt herself begin to flush.

"Yeah, but can you really blame them for following you around, Maggie darlin'?" he drawled.

"Watching your every move? Waiting for you to glance their way and throw them a crumb or two?"

His eyes were smoldering with an azure-tinged flame, and his voice was so warmly charged with erotic intent, she could swear she felt their combined tingling heat straight down to the soles of her feet.

Her mouth went dry. Her abdominal muscles began to tighten.

"Hell, half the time I'm tempted to do the same thing myself," he said huskily. "And I don't even cover the entertainment news."

Her heart started to pound. She tightened her clasp on both the bags and the boom box and leaned just a little closer.

"So why do you keep holding yourself back?" she asked. "After all, they say a little temptation can be good for the soul."

His gaze burned into hers.

"Yeah, but they say it can also lead you straight into damnation if you're not careful," he said, sounding huskier still.

"Is that what you're so afraid of, Jake?" she asked softly. "That I'll lead you straight into damnation? Because you have my word, I'd never intentionally do anything to hurt you. *Never*."

He laughed. The sound was so low and undeniably sensual, it made her knees go weak and her stomach turn a flipflop.

"Yeah, well, sorry to disillusion you, Maggie darlin', but your reputation suggests otherwise. You see, the way I hear it, you're a wild-at-heart heiress with a passion for living on a much grander scale than the rest of us mere mortals. That makes you a natural-born heartbreaker in my book."

He reached past her for the last two bags in the Jeep. His arm lightly brushed against her shoulder, sending a shower of fire-laced sparks shooting straight down her spine. She tried to resist the urge to shiver, but couldn't.

"And as for always being stalked by the tabloids," he went on, "I think we both know that you sealed your fate as a bona fide media sensation long ago. Say around the same time you poured that bottle of pink bubble bath into a public fountain and decided to take a moonlight swim with a few of your girlfriends?"

Then he turned and headed back into the cabin.

"Now, that's *exactly* what I was talking about," she called after him. "I mean, I was seventeen years old and still in high school, for pity's sake. Name one thing that I've done recently."

"Just one?" he yelled back. "Hell, I could probably find hundreds if I scanned a few of the back issues of the *Sentinel*."

Still grinning, she followed him inside the cabin and dropped the bags and boom box on the kitchen floor next to the table.

"Just one, thank you," she said. "And something post-college too, since I was still a little rebellious even then."

Save 85% Off The Cover Price on 4 *Loveswept* Romances

Get 4 Loveswept Romances

For The *Low Introductory Price*

Of Just $1.99*

*Plus shipping & handling, sales tax in New York, and GST Canada.

Titles you
receive ma[y]
differ fro[m]
those show[n]
here, b[ut]
will [be]
the late[st]
Loveswe[pt]
selection[s]

No Risk. No obligation to purchase. No commitment.

He glanced at her out of the corner of his eye as he unpacked the groceries.

"Okay," he said. "How about your torrid love affair with Charlie Darnell two years ago? After you dumped him, the poor guy was so broken up, he had to take a year off just to recover."

She laughed and started to unpack the bags she'd brought in.

"Some reporter you've turned out to be, Jake Wilder. Charlie took a year off because he'd done four big-budget films straight and needed a vacation. And just for your information, I never 'dumped' Charlie, because we were never anything more than just good friends to begin with. All the time the *Sentinel* claimed that we were dating, he was only helping me get the financial backing I needed to open Pet Haven."

"Good friends, huh? Isn't that what you said about Senator McNichols?" Jake asked, transferring the canned goods to the cupboard above the stove. "Only, as I recall, *he* seemed to think you two were a lot more."

"Yes, but Todd's judgment calls haven't been all that sound lately, have they?"

Jake looked thoughtful for a moment, then transferred the rest of their food to the cupboard.

"You've got me there," he murmured. "So what's this Pet Haven place you keep talking about?"

She smiled and unloaded another bag. "It's a privately funded animal shelter I cofounded in Marin County. We rescue abused and abandoned pets, nurse them back to health if they need it, then try to find them good homes. We work with strays mostly, although we get a few who've been abused by their owners. We operate strictly by donation, which is why Charlie was such a big help to us when we first got started."

She carried a stack of their new clothes into the bedroom area, separated them into two piles, then tucked them into different drawers of the small dresser next to the bed before returning to the kitchen.

"The public response has been positive so far," she went on. "We have five full-time volunteer staff members, not including myself. We're hoping to open a second refuge in L.A. County sometime early next year, which I'll probably run, at least in the beginning."

"Another one of those dirty jobs that you can't help doing?" he teased.

He folded his arms over his chest, then leaned against the edge of the sink to give her another one of his bad-boy grins.

She held his gaze for a moment, feeling herself begin to flush all over again.

"Yeah, but it's not nearly as much fun as some others I could mention," she teased back.

She brushed past him and went out the back door to check on the generator.

❖━━━━━❖

Two hours later, Jake sat slumped in the easy chair, too wound up to sleep and too distracted by the rhythmic sound of Maggie's breathing to read one of the paperbacks they'd picked up in the supermarket.

Her lack of sleep had finally caught up with her after she'd gotten the generator running—if he hadn't seen her in action with the wrench himself, he'd have never believed it—and she'd climbed into bed and fallen asleep after their dinner of canned chicken noodle soup and fresh fruit.

Just as he'd threatened he'd do, Jake had strung a piece of nylon cord from the window to the floor lamp, then tossed one of the extra blankets across it, hoping the illusion of privacy would cool down his overheated libido.

The only problem was, it didn't seem to be working.

He was all too aware of Maggie sleeping on the other side of their make-believe wall, just as he was all too aware of how her slender body would look in the pajama top . . . all sensual curves and long, tanned legs that not even the innocence of flannel could disguise.

If he closed his eyes, he could almost imagine her snuggling close to him on the oversize easy chair . . . lightly massaging his shoulders with her fingertips . . . whispering naughty but infinitely pleasurable suggestions in his ear . . . then pressing her lips against his abdomen, then his chest, then his chin . . . before straddling his hips and easing herself onto him to take them both for the ride of their lives.

Jake drew a slow, ragged breath, held it for a moment, then exhaled.

Aw, hell, what was the use? he asked himself in mounting frustration. He might as well just surrender to her now and get it over with.

They were supposed to stay together at the cabin for five whole days, perhaps even seven. At the rate he was going, he'd be lucky if he made it another hour without losing his already tenuous grip on his sanity.

SEVEN

Twenty-four hours later, with the unbearably erotic strains of a Chris Isaak CD serenading them from the boom box in the living room, Jake sat across from Maggie at the table in the kitchen, playing their fifth game of poker. Her myriad talents apparently knew few limitations, and she'd easily won the last four hands, plus the game of Trivial Pursuit she'd conned him into before dinner.

Jake had spent the day trying his damnedest to avoid a too-close-for-emotional-comfort contact with her, and he was exhausted from the effort. As a matter of fact, his resolve not to give in to his desire for her had already weakened to the point where one more twinkle of her sexy hazel eyes would likely have him surrendering both his body and his soul without so much as an additional murmur of protest.

What's more, every fiber of his being told him she knew it too.

"But Joe Montana was the best quarterback the 49ers ever had," she said, quickly sorting through her recently dealt hand. "I can't believe you don't like him. I'll open with a dime."

She tossed two nickels into the kitty in the center of the table.

He regarded her a moment over the edge of his cards and slowly smiled. Her face was free of makeup, and she'd pulled her long, honey-colored hair back into a ponytail. She looked vulnerable and much younger than her twenty-seven years but still so damned beautiful he couldn't concentrate on anything but her.

"I'll see your ten," Jake said, sliding a dime over to join her ante. "And I never said I didn't like Montana. Only that I didn't think he was as good in his last few seasons with the Kansas City Chiefs as he'd once been with the 49ers."

She shrugged. "Maybe so. But even on his worst day on the field, Joe was still better than the best of the rest. What's more, he's about the sexiest-looking pro quarterback of all time."

She glanced at him and grinned. "Although he's not nearly as handsome as you, darling."

Her voice was so playfully seductive, it made his pulse start to race.

"In fact," she added, dropping her voice even lower, "I can't think of a single man who even comes close . . . even with that rugged mountain-man look you've got going there."

Jake held her gaze for a moment longer, feeling his body tighten and grow hard. He started to flush and rubbed his palm over the stubble of his un-shaved face.

"Is your hand really that bad, Maggie darlin', that you have to resort to blatantly insincere flattery in order to win?"

Her grin deepened. "Who says I'm insincere?"

"Uh-huh. How many cards do you want?"

"Two."

"Fine. The dealer'll take one."

He dealt out two cards from the deck and pushed them over to her, then dealt another for himself. He slid the deck onto the table and studied his hand for a moment, trying to focus on the game, but it was no use. Hard as he tried, he couldn't seem to help himself from casting quick glances at her over the top of his cards—just as he couldn't seem to stop fantasizing about tossing the damned cards aside and reaching across the table to pull her closer to him. Or to stop fantasizing about tilting her chin up to kiss her sweet lips . . . slowly and deeply, until she melted against him and her tongue sought out his in an equally erotic caress that would leave him trembling and harder still.

He couldn't stop fantasizing about letting him-self love her even though he knew that he'd be a damned fool if he ever followed through on any of his libidinous thoughts.

"I'll raise you another nickel," Maggie said, tossing in the coin. "And then I call."

He drew a slow, ragged breath and tried to force his attention back to the game.

"Here's the nickel." He added his money to the pot. "And here's my hand." He laid out his cards. "Well, what do you know?" He smiled. "Three sixes. I think I got you beat this time, Maggie darlin'."

Her hazel eyes started to sparkle and dance.

"Afraid you didn't even come close," she said, laying out her own cards. "I've got a full house. Queens over eights."

He shook his head and leaned back in his chair. "Five hands in a row? I think I'm being set up. You're obviously some Las Vegas cardsharp who merely moonlights as an heiress."

She laughed. "Hey, is it my fault that you're not paying attention to the game?" she teased.

He met her gaze. *Oh, absolutely*, he thought, giving her a grin.

She reached for the card he'd discarded during the last hand and turned it over.

"Why, look," she said. "You even threw away a six. If you'd kept it, you'd have probably won."

He shrugged and drained the last of his decaffeinated coffee. "Yeah, well, I guess that means I'd better quit while I'm down only a buck fifty."

She looked disappointed. "But don't you want

to try to win your money back? We could play double or nothing. I'd even let you cheat this time."

He shook his head. "Better not chance it. Truth is, between the Trivial Pursuit and the cards, I'm tired of playing games."

She stared at him for a moment, then gave him a smile so downright appealing, it warmed some cold, dark spot deep inside him. She reached across the table and took his hand, wrapping her fingers around his palm to give him a gentle squeeze.

He drew a sharp breath. Her touch was like fire; it turned his blood to liquefied heat and set his nerve endings deliciously aflame. Then his heart started to pound as if he'd just received an intravenous injection of pure adrenaline.

"So am I," she said huskily. "Terribly tired of playing this silly little game of ours."

She leaned in a little closer. "So tell me, darling," she murmured. "Just what do you suggest we do about it?"

"Well, I . . ."

His mouth went dry. His abdominal muscles began to constrict.

"I, ah, guess we'd better call it a night," he murmured back.

He slipped his hand from hers and stood up. Then he crossed over and turned off the CD player before moving on to the bedroom as fast as his feet could carry him.

"You're kidding, right?" Maggie asked. "You

want to go to sleep? *Now?* I mean, it's not even eight o'clock, for pity's sake."

He opened the bottom dresser drawer and removed the red and black checked flannel pajamas. He tossed the pants onto the bed and its matching top over to the easy chair, which was where Maggie would be sleeping, since they'd agreed to take turns using the bed.

"Yeah, well, days are shorter in the mountains," he mumbled. "Something about the reduced amount of oxygen in the atmosphere. I don't remember all the details."

"Jake . . . you do realize you're not making any sense at all, don't you?"

He retrieved the dark-colored woolen blanket he'd used as a room divider the night before and draped it back over the cord still strung from the wall to the metal floor lamp. From the blanket's fraying top to its ragged bottom, Jake figured it hung ten feet across by five feet down. It wasn't much, but it would probably be the only thing keeping his libido under control from here on out.

That and a hastily murmured prayer or two.

"All the more reason for us to call it a night, don't you think?" he tossed over his shoulder.

Maggie sighed and turned off the light in the kitchen. "Oh, what's the use?" Then she moved to the other side of the blanket.

Jake's fingers fumbled with the buttons on his shirt. "Look, you don't have to go to sleep if you don't want to," he told her. "I'm planning to finish the book I started last night. You could do the same with one of the ones we bought at the supermarket."

"Trust me, Jake," she said, giving him a short laugh. "I really don't think *that* would be such a good idea just now."

He could hear her peeling off her clothes. His heart started to thud even faster. His gaze moved toward the blanket like a piece of metal drawn toward a powerful magnet, but it was too dark for him to see even the suggestion of her silhouette from the other side.

"Why's that?" he asked, shrugging off his shirt. He tossed it onto the dresser.

"All I bought were romances. Large, thick, juicy ones filled with sexy stories of ruggedly handsome and virile men . . . I figure I've got enough problems as it is without overstimulating my imagination," she grumbled under her breath.

He grinned. He knew exactly what she meant, although his own imagination didn't need any additional stimulation in order for it to overheat.

"Then try reading one of mine," he suggested. "They're nice, erotically uninspiring murder mysteries."

And so unengrossing thus far that he hadn't even made it past the first chapter.

He pulled off his jeans and boxer shorts and tossed them onto the dresser to join his shirt. He reached for the pajama bottoms and pulled them on.

"That's not the point," she said.

"Then what is?"

"That you're being . . . oh! Just ridiculous about this whole thing! I know that you feel something for me, Jake. But rather than see where it might lead us, you run away each time things get a little too emotionally hot for you to handle. It's driving me nuts."

"But we've already been through this. We both agreed that we're simply not right for each other, that we could have no possible future together. That's why we decided the only sensible thing for us to do would be to keep our relationship strictly platonic."

"But who wants to be sensible about love, Jake? Can you please tell me that?"

He heard a fluttering sound and glanced over in time to see the blanket fall to the floor in a crumpled heap. Maggie stood in the shadows next to the fallen blanket, looking more beautiful than ever before. Her hair hung loose and flowing around her shoulders, and the pajama top ended just above her knee, seductively hinting at every sensuous curve of her body.

He drew another sharp breath. "Maggie . . . I . . . really wish you hadn't done that."

She gave him a soft smile. "I had no choice," she said, stepping over the blanket. "Joshua may have been willing to wait for seven whole days for the walls of Jericho to tumble, but I can't."

Before he could stop her, she'd crossed over to

the bed and wound her arms tightly around his neck. Then she pulled herself against him until her breasts were crushed to his bare chest and his ability to resist her had finally snapped.

"Make love to me, Jake," she murmured breathlessly. "Please. Before we both lose our minds."

He softly moaned, then lowered his head and brushed his lips over hers, lightly at first, then building to a fierceness of longing and need that rocked him to his very foundation.

"Too late," he muttered hoarsely, gathering her in his arms to pull her closer. "I'm afraid I've already lost mine."

Weaving her suddenly trembling fingers through Jake's thick dark hair, and returning his kiss with a passion that seemed to explode from somewhere deep inside her, Maggie felt as though she'd lost her mind too.

After all, what other explanation could there be but temporary insanity? She was literally throwing herself at the man, offering him both her body and her heart, when he'd made it clear right from the beginning that he wasn't interested in having either. What's more, she was so afraid—terrified, actually—that he was going to push her away from him again when the part of her brain that was still rational enough to worry about such things told her that she should be more afraid that he might take her up on her foolish offer. If they made love, as she so desperately prayed that they would, the most she could ever hope for would be a blissfully sweet but short-lived affair, which wouldn't be nearly enough to satisfy her.

Not when she knew in her heart that she wanted so much more from him than a few sweet days or even weeks spent wrapped in each other's arms.

Not when she knew she needed a lifetime of his sexy-as-sin *Maggie darlin'*'s and his divinely sensuous, toe-curling kisses.

Not when she flat-out loved him so much that just thinking about him made her tremble.

Hell, even if Jake decided he loved her back and wanted to pursue something more long-term, she knew that his career, the quest for the next great story, would always come first with him. Knowing that she would always come second would never be enough for her. So why . . . ?

His tongue started to move over hers, stroking and teasing, arousing her already stimulated senses with a slow erotic massage so intensely pleasurable that she was sure it would short-circuit her brain.

She moaned and pulled him closer, deciding right then and there that she didn't care about the consequences of letting herself love him.

She didn't care about anything at all except how good it felt to kiss him . . . and to hold him . . . and to know without a shadow of a doubt that he wanted her, loved her, as much as she did him.

Whatever the ultimate price for the pleasure of making love with him might be, at that moment she felt certain it would be well worth the investment of both her heart and soul.

Jake slowly slid his hands down her back, scorching through the lightweight flannel of her pajama top with his touch like an acetylene torch through a bolt of silk. His hands lingered over her buttocks for a moment, sending fire-laced tremors rocketing through to her core from the heat of his palms against the flannel.

Slowly breaking off their kiss, he eased his hands down her upper thighs to grasp the bottom of the pajama top.

"You feel so damned good, Maggie darlin'," he murmured huskily against her ear.

He started to nuzzle her neck, alternating between the brush of his lips and the rake of his tongue along her fevered skin. Each kiss, each caress, created a more deliciously titillating sensation than the one before it.

"Better than I'd ever fantasized you'd feel pressed against me," he added in a breathless whisper. "And believe me, in the last forty-eight hours I've fantasized about making love to you a lot."

Her heart began to thud wildly in her chest.

"But why keep fantasizing when you can have the real thing, darling?" she asked in a voice as husky as his had been. "When we both could?"

She loosened her grip on his hair and glided her

hands down his back, marveling at the strength and power of his tightly corded muscles, awed by how smooth and warm his bare skin felt beneath her fingers.

She decided she liked Jake's body. She liked its hardness, its overwhelming aura of maleness that emanated from somewhere deep inside him. She liked the musky scent of him, how it was tempered only by soap and baby powder. She liked how he tasted of coffee and the pound cake they'd had for dessert.

She liked the way his soft chest hair bristled against her cheek when he held her close to him.

She especially liked the way he had of making her feel so utterly and completely feminine each time he looked at her.

She felt herself flush. Her breath caught in her throat.

"Or were you planning to disappoint us both by making another mad dash for the nearest exit?" she added, half afraid that he might mumble another apology and push her away again.

"Not this time," he murmured, sounding huskier still. "Hell, the whole damn mountain can crumble around us from the earthquake of the century, and it wouldn't be enough to stop us. Nothing is as powerful as what I feel for you right now . . . *nothing.*"

He flicked his tongue over her right earlobe, then pulled it into his mouth, caressing its tip, teasing her with a gentle rake of his teeth along its edge until he bombarded her overloaded senses with more electrically charged shivers that made her knees go absolutely weak.

She shuddered against him.

"But . . . what about that reporter's survival manual you put so much stock in?" she asked breathlessly. "The one that said it was so downright dangerous for you even to kiss me?"

He gave her a laugh so steeped in sensual heat, she was afraid her bones might begin to melt.

"Oh, that?" he asked.

"Yes, that. As I recall, you spent a lot of time quoting the damn thing to me."

"Yeah, well, I won't be quoting it to you any longer. In fact, I decided to throw the book away. I figured I might as well give in to the temptation the way you suggested . . . even if I am pretty damn certain it'll only end up killing me in the long run."

He started to roll up her pajama top, one slow, careful quarter-inch at a time, sliding both fingertips and nails along her skin with a touch that was positively incendiary, only to linger again when he came to her buttocks. He splayed his fingers across the white cotton panties she'd purchased back at the Real McCoy's, and gave her bottom a gentle squeeze.

Heat seared through the thin fabric to brand her skin, maybe even a bit of her soul.

"After all, what do I really have to lose?" His voice was rough with emotion. "I've been wanting you so damn bad that it's been killing me anyway . . . one slow cell of my body at a time."

Then, with a deliberate sensuality that she was certain was designed for the single purpose of making her come undone, he started to trace a fire-streaked path around the lacy edge of her panties with his fingertips, teasing her unmercifully with his featherlike touch until she burned hard and strong for him, assaulting her senses until her abdominal muscles started to constrict and her mouth went dry, tormenting her with his too-soft touches until she could only cling to him, craving more than just the light brush of his hands against her body.

"Do you . . . promise?" she asked.

She glided her hands around his sides to touch his chest, feeling the soft hair there rustle beneath her fingers.

"Because if you stop now, Jake Wilder," she added hoarsely, "I may just kill you myself."

He laughed again. "And I do believe you mean it, darlin'," he said. "Although you've got no need to worry. I don't plan to stop making love to you until we've both gotten our fill . . . which for me may probably be sometime in the next century or so."

"Same here," she whispered in a voice that even to her own ears revealed far too much emotion than was probably safe.

She arched her hips toward him, trying to mold

herself against him, wanting to fuse her body with his.

As though he sensed what she needed, he gently grasped her buttocks and pulled her closer until their hips hit the proper alignment and she could feel his arousal pressing against her. He was hard. So very hard. Another shudder racked her body.

"It's going to be so good between us, Maggie darlin'," he said, breathing in her ear. "You feel so ready, so hot right now, I may just burst into flames from holding you."

Still bracing her backside with his hands, he slowly rubbed her against his growing hardness until liquid heat began to pool in her lower abdomen and she began to ache from the want of him. She gasped his name and began to move her hips in a slow, sensual rhythm that matched his own.

"Then let's . . . just burn up together," she whispered back.

She kissed his neck, his chin, his cheek, feeling his two-day stubble roughly brush against her skin with each kiss, and not caring if she ended up with the world's worst case of whisker burn or not.

"We could fuse our two flames into one," she said, wetting that adorable cleft in his chin with the tip of her tongue. "Right here. Right now."

He groaned deep in his throat. His mouth sought out hers, and he kissed her again, deeper this time, more frenzied too. It was as though his tolerance for additional foreplay had finally begun to wane as much as hers already had.

God, how she wanted him, how she wanted to feel him shudder beneath her fingertips the way he made her shudder. It had been a long time since she'd been so intimate with a man and even longer since it had felt so good, so incredibly right.

Feeling gloriously wanton, heady with desire, she slowly glided her hand down his front to the elastic waistband of his pajamas as the kiss deepened, inching closer to the unmistakable outline of his arousal. She wanted to touch him. Had to touch him. It was a need as fundamental as breathing and twice as compelling.

Her abdominal muscles constricted again as she slid her palm over the bulge in his pajamas. Her hand started to tremble. He felt larger than she'd expected. Almost too large.

She hesitated for a moment, then began to caress him, gently massaging his erection through the pajamas with the palm of her hand. Then she steadily increased the tempo of her movements until he closed his eyes and slid his hand over hers to press her palm closer, whispering little words of pure masculine pleasure as her stroking became more directed, more sensual.

She started to flush, feeling almost embarrassed at how bold she had become, but she felt pleasure, and joy, too, at the power she had over him.

"Maggie darlin'." He moaned softly, easing her hand away. "When you touch me like that, I do believe I could fall hopelessly in love with you."

She felt her heart skip a beat. "So what's holding you back?" she asked.

He didn't answer her. Instead, he maneuvered her around to sit on the bed. His eyes glittered with a fevered intensity that she knew must match her own, but along with the desire he felt for her burned other emotions, conflicting emotions like pain and fear, which logic told her had little to do with their relationship although she knew it would affect them nonetheless.

Perhaps even destroy them.

"Jake . . . please talk to me," she whispered. "I need to know how you feel." She wanted to know even though his answer could very well break her heart into a million unsalvageable pieces.

"Feel about what?" he asked. He knelt down on the floor beside the bed.

"About me . . . about us."

He gave her a crooked sort of smile. "Are words really all that necessary?" he asked.

"Well . . . yes."

He gently cupped her face in his hands and kissed her, sliding his tongue past her parted lips to engage her own in an amorous dance that made her abdominal muscles constrict again, almost painfully this time. She could feel him start to unfasten the plastic buttons on her pajama top and shivered from the fiery brush of his fingers against her already fevered flesh.

"You bring me to my knees, darlin'," he said.

He pressed his lips against the hollow between her breasts, singeing her skin, making her tremble.

"You make me feel things I told myself I never wanted to feel again."

"You . . . have the same effect on me," she murmured back.

She ran her hands through his hair, loving the way it slid between her fingers like strands of black silk.

"You look at me, and I feel goose bumps spring up all over my body," she said. "You kiss me, and I feel like my bones have turned to putty. We're so good together, Jake. So unbelievably right."

She traced her fingertips along his ears. "And not just sexually," she said, "but in dozens of other ways too. Like the way we worked together down at the Real McCoy's and back with Raymond in Todd's room. We're a perfect team."

He hesitated a moment, then undid another button of her top, taking his time, as though undressing her were something he'd thought a lot about and didn't want to rush the job.

"Don't . . . expect more from me than I can give you, Maggie," he said quietly. "All I really have to offer you is tonight. Maybe tomorrow. Just a small fragment in time together, really. If that's not good enough for you, well, maybe we'd better stop right now."

His words stung her. He may not have been running away from her physically anymore, but emotionally he seemed to be doing the hundred-yard dash.

She sighed and leaned toward him, resting her hands on his bare shoulders for a moment before lightly massaging his tense, tight muscles.

"I think the real question here, darling, is whether our 'small fragment of time together' as you call it, is going to be good enough for *you*."

Then she kissed him, slowly and deliberately, caressing his tongue with her own, wanting to show him how wrong he was to keep fighting what they felt for each other, wanting to drug his senses with all-consuming desire for her as much as he'd drugged hers.

He groaned, then she felt his fingers entangle themselves in her hair and tighten around it, pulling her just a little closer to where he still knelt on the floor next to the bed.

Wanting to memorize every curve and angle of his face, she ran her fingertips along it, feeling the stubble from his beard bristle beneath her, taking delight in the tremor that shook him as her kisses became more wanton, more erotic.

He moved his hands through the opening of the pajama top and began touching her breasts. He held them in his palms, stroking them gently for a moment, then he squeezed the nipples between his thumb and forefinger, molding them into two stiffened peaks until the ache from wanting more of him became almost unbearable.

She broke off the kiss. "Jake . . . I don't think I can take any more of this. I need you. *Now*."

His gaze locked with hers. His eyes had darkened to the deep blue of the sky right before a storm hits, when even the air itself seemed to be charged with electricity and pulsating with raw energy. Then he smiled and started to remove her top.

"I bet when you were a kid you couldn't wait for Christmas to open your presents either."

His tone was lightly teasing, but there could be no mistaking the undercurrent of raw desire just beneath its surface.

She nodded and shrugged out of her pajamas. The top slid to the floor.

"My—my parents used to lock all my presents up in the pantry downstairs," she said. "It was a complete waste of time. I'd always have every one of my gifts unwrapped and well used by Christmas Eve."

He gave her that bad-boy grin of his, a grin so warm it aroused her even more than the searing sensual heat from his touch.

"You know, Maggie darlin', some people consider patience a virtue."

He stroked her breasts again, kneading them gently with the palms of his hand, sending wave after glorious wave of pleasure crashing around her until she felt as if she couldn't breathe.

"And I promise you," he added. "When we finally make love, it's going to be well worth the wait for both of us."

His lips brushed against her breasts, first one, then the other, following each brief kiss with a flick of his tongue across her sensitized nipples that sent dozens of white-hot quivers tumbling through her.

"I know," she said, moaning. "But . . ."

"But what?"

"I don't know how long I can last." She squeezed her eyes closed for a moment as another shudder racked her body. "It's . . . it's been a long time for me, Jake."

He slowly rubbed his thumbs across her tightened nipples. "How long?"

She blushed. "That's . . . really none of your business," she said, and gave him a short laugh.

"How long?" he asked again, tilting up her chin, forcing her to open her eyes and look at him. "Tell me."

She met his passion-streaked gaze. "Well, I . . . how long has it been for you?" she countered.

He smiled. "So long that the condom I've been carrying around in my wallet in case I ever got lucky is probably covered with cobwebs by now."

She relaxed, feeling relieved to know that making love wasn't a casual thing with him either.

"It's . . . been a little over four years for me," she told him.

He studied her face for a moment. "So are you sure we're going to be okay?"

She tugged on his shoulders, trying to pull him into the bed with her. "Jake, believe me. I've never been more sure about anything in my entire life."

He pushed her hands away from him and pressed them against the mattress. "Yeah, but we can't allow our libidos to go totally crazy here, Maggie. I mean, we're an hour away from the nearest drugstore and a fresh supply of condoms, and I want you so damned bad, I can't promise how careful I'll be."

His expression was intense, almost tortured. His eyes glittered with unchecked passion.

She felt herself blush as she realized the reason for his hesitation. "We, ah, don't have to worry about my getting pregnant, if that's what's troubling you. My hormones . . . well, they've been a little out of whack lately. My gynecologist's been giving me these shots every three months. She says they're more reliable than traditional birth control pills."

His expression relaxed. "Smart lady, your doctor," he murmured. "Remind me to send her a thank-you card when we get back home."

He eased her back on the bed, running his hands down her body in long, measured strokes, lovingly touching her neck and shoulders, massaging her breasts, caressing her abdomen. Then he slid his hand between her legs to touch her through her cotton panties, gently rubbing his thumb back and forth until she shuddered against him. Liquid heat began to swirl through her lower abdomen, a heat so intensely consuming that all she could do was writhe against his hand.

"Just . . . how . . . close are you, Maggie darlin', to coming apart?" he whispered softly.

His voice was rough and filled with so much hunger, so much need, she found herself trembling.

She gasped. "I'm . . . close." One more stroke of his hand would send her careening over the edge.

He laughed. Then he grasped the lacy border of her panties and slowly tugged them down. She raised herself slightly, feeling his fingertips brush a hot path down her hips as he tugged off her underwear. He tossed the panties to the floor next to him, then glided his palms up her legs to part her thighs.

"Then why fight it?" he whispered.

He positioned himself between her thighs, pulling her legs up until her feet rested on his broad shoulders, then tugging her hips closer to the edge of the bed.

"Just let yourself go," he said.

He brushed his lips against her knee, making her skin sizzle and her body ache to feel his hardness buried deep inside her, then he slowly moved up her leg to the juncture of her thighs, marking the path with the soft brush of his lips against her skin.

She gasped when she felt him rake his tongue across her, skillfully parting the folds of her femininity, edging closer and closer to her tightened nub of desire until she thought for sure that she would pass out from the sheer carnal pleasure he was unleashing inside her.

"Jake . . ." she whispered, clutching his hair in her fingers to bring him closer, pressing her heels against his shoulders, needing more from him than she could ever put into words.

He slid his hands under her hips to angle her closer to his mouth, then he continued to pleasure her, leisurely, as though all he wanted in the world was to taste her, to love her, and to expect absolutely nothing in return.

This wasn't fair, dammit, she thought in frustration, that he could shift the balance of power between them so suddenly and so completely, that he could make her feel so desired and yet so damnably vulnerable all at the same time.

He slid his finger inside her wetness, moving it deeper and harder as he increased the rhythm of his tongue against her until she couldn't maintain her control. It felt so good. His hands, his lips, his tongue. All of him.

"That's it, darlin'," he whispered, increasing the rhythm of his stroking. "Come apart for me. Just let it happen."

She gasped his name, chanted it like a mantra, arching her hips closer to him as the fireburst swept her up in its power. It took her higher and higher, to the stars and beyond, until her release overtook her in a blinding explosion of sensation unlike anything she'd ever experienced before. She didn't stop trembling until she'd floated back down to earth . . . where she found Jake lying beside her on the bed, holding her close.

EIGHT

Jake knew he was damned the moment his gaze locked with hers, knew that the battle he'd been waging to protect his heart had been lost without so much as a murmur of protest on his part.

Lord, he thought, stroking her hair. He hadn't expected that bringing her to a climax could feel so good. He hadn't expected that feeling her control shatter beneath his mouth could engage his emotions so completely, even supersede his own powerful need for release.

She gave him a shy, soft smile, full of tenderness and caring.

It sent his heart pounding out of control.

"Shame on you, Jake Wilder," she said hoarsely. "You didn't play fair."

He smiled back and pressed his lips against her forehead. Her skin felt damp with perspiration, flushed with heat.

"Funny," he teased. "I didn't hear you complaining a few moments ago."

"And you won't now," she said. "You were wonderful, darling." She started to blush. "No one has ever made it . . . happen . . . for me that way before."

Her voice was shadowed with raw emotion. Its sound wrapped around his heart, squeezing like a vise, until he vowed that he'd make it happen for her that way over and over again until she finally became bored with the routine.

"But you promised me we would burn up together," she reminded him.

She glided her hand across his chest, drawing an erotic circle around his left nipple with the tip of her index finger, then rubbing lightly across its tightened bud until he shuddered.

"Instead, I was the one who went up in flames," she said, "while you stayed cool and in control."

His arousal strained against the fabric of his pajama bottoms. He wanted her. Now. He was so ready that he could barely maintain his grasp on his self-control. Every nerve ending in his tense, tight body demanded that he tear off his pajamas, push her back on the bed, wrap her long, tanned legs around his hips, and bury himself deep inside her slick, feminine heat.

"Trust me, darlin'," he said. He shifted slightly to rub his arousal against her hip. "I'm . . . anything . . . but in control."

"I—"

He felt her shudder, then she rolled in to him until they were lying belly to belly, hips to hips, until his arousal was cradled within her thighs with only his clothes separating their fevered flesh.

"Then why didn't you . . . ?" She seemed to struggle with the words.

"You were so close, I just couldn't help myself," he said, brushing her perspiration-dampened hair off her forehead.

Just as he couldn't help himself from wanting to watch her face as the pleasure overtook her, knowing it was his touch, the feel of his tongue that made her body fall apart. He'd never felt this way about a woman before, felt such an overwhelming need to stake ownership, to claim her for his own that the thought of any other man touching her was enough to make him lose his mind.

"Besides, I'm a big man, darlin'," he said softly. "And you felt so tight. I thought we should take things slow so I didn't hurt you."

She moved against him, arching her hips until she rubbed against his arousal. He drew a sharp breath as a spasm rocked him.

"But it hurts even more not to feel you inside me," she said.

She slowly slid her hand down between their bodies and tugged on the elastic waistband of his pajamas. Her fingertips sizzled against his skin, making him shiver, electrifying his soul.

"Don't fight it anymore, darling," she whispered, pushing him onto his back and sliding his pajamas down his hips. "Isn't that what you told me? Not to fight the feelings?"

He squeezed his eyes closed and lifted his hips, letting her peel off his pajamas, shuddering when they rolled past his erection.

"I . . . said . . . you should just let it happen."

He kicked his pants aside and opened his eyes to meet her gaze. Need, desire, burned in the depths of her eyes along with another emotion he knew he needed from her even more, even though it did have the power to terrify him. He started to tremble.

"Then let it happen, Jake," she said.

She pulled him on top of her, arching herself up to his hips until the rigid tip of his shaft nudged against her welcoming heat.

"Just let yourself go . . . right this second . . . inside me."

He eased his fingers into her wetness, first one, then two. She felt hot . . . tight. So tight, he was still afraid he might hurt her if he lost control. He probed a little deeper, moved his fingers a little faster, until she gasped his name and clutched at his shoulders, telling him with her soft whimpers that she was as ready for him as he was for her.

His heart thudded wildly. He slowly removed his fingers and guided himself inside her, taking his time, fighting the urge to thrust himself deep and hard into her even though the walls of her body seemed to constrict around him, pulling him closer, sending his senses reeling with a rush of possessiveness unlike any he'd ever felt before.

"Please tell me that you want me, Maggie darlin'." He moved a little faster, a little deeper. "Tell me that you need me, that you need this as much as I do."

Her fingers dug into his shoulders. She wrapped her legs around his thighs and hugged him to her.

"I . . . I want you, Jake," she whispered in a voice as rough with desire as his own. "I need you . . . need this . . . more than life."

He groaned and gave one good thrust until he was fully inside her. Later they could take their time, he decided, pulling out to thrust into her again. Later they could savor the tastes and textures of their bodies. Now he wanted to stake his claim on her soul . . . make her his. For now and for always.

He kissed her neck, feeling her pulse flutter wildly beneath his lips.

"I need you . . . need this . . . too," he whispered back. "You feel so damned good that I can't hold on much longer."

"Then why even try?" she asked, moving faster, squeezing him tighter with her muscles until he could only shudder into her. "Just let yourself come apart, darling."

"Maggie . . ." He clutched her tighter.

"I want you, Jake," she said again, seeming to know without his asking that he needed the sound of her voice to take him over the edge and send him spiraling home. "I want only you."

He moaned her name again and intensified his thrusts. So close. So close.

"I *need* you too," she said, her voice sounding more like a hoarse cry. "I need your passion, your love, so much that it scares me . . . oh, Jake. I love you."

He tried to block out the last part, but couldn't. Her words burned inside him until his control shattered. He'd wanted desperately to believe that they were only having sex, only filling an intense physical need that they felt for each other and nothing more. He'd wanted to believe that he could spend one night with her and be satisfied enough the next day to let her go. But he couldn't. He knew better.

He loved her.

Heaven help him.

He was damned, and there was nothing he could do to save himself.

A loud clanking noise like a wrench being tapped none too gently against a heavy metal object jarred Maggie awake shortly before eleven the next day. The annoyingly intrusive sounds were coming from outside, where, unless she missed her guess, Jake was trying—and none too successfully, at that—to fix the generator.

Unable to mask a grin—he'd probably demolish the machine for good if she didn't go out there and stop him first—she threw off the covers and scrambled out of bed. Pushing her hair out of her eyes, she ran across the still-crumpled wall of Jericho to grab her jeans and shirt from the easy chair.

Poor baby, she thought, quickly getting dressed. He should have awakened her rather than attempt to make the repairs by himself. After all, there were some things that Jake was just plain clueless about, like fixing a malfunctioning electrical generator for one—and the depth of his feelings for her, for another.

She hugged herself, taking joy at remembering the hours they'd spent together the night before, kissing and touching and loving each other until sheer exhaustion had finally taken its toll on their bodies, and they'd drifted off to sleep, holding each other close.

Loving Jake, having him love her, had felt so good, it had been beyond perfection, yet she'd still sensed his emotional hesitation even at the height of their intimacy. It was as though he were holding back a part of himself each time they touched, holding back the best part, the part she needed most from him—his heart, his unqualified love and trust.

She sighed. She knew she'd taken an emotional gamble when she'd asked him to make love to her, probably the biggest gamble of her life. Because she knew someone had hurt him, cut him clear through to the bone, making him afraid to love. Even now she still wasn't certain if he was finally willing to surrender to what he felt for her and return her love with the same passion that she felt for him . . . or if he was planning to erect another wall between them, making this one stronger and more unbreachable than the last had been.

The clanking grew louder; it was quickly followed by a colorful expletive. Grinning again, she slipped on her sneakers and headed for the back door.

Jake was behind the cabin, crouched down next to the weathered generator. His forehead was furrowed, and streaks of axle grease lined his cheek.

"Beating the generator into submission, darling, isn't going to help," she teased. "Now, why don't you hand me the wrench before you break the damned thing completely and we have to resort to candlelight for the duration of our stay?"

He slowly looked up and met her gaze. That's when she knew that she'd lost the gamble. She'd lost him. Whatever temporary hold she may have once managed to place on his heart had apparently snapped, because the emotional barriers were back up again, the barriers that were so insurmountable this time that not even a hundred blasts from Joshua's mighty trumpet could likely crack them.

She felt her smile begin to fade.

"I'm sorry if I woke you," he said.

His voice sounded so polite, it nearly broke her heart.

"No problem," she said.

He rose to his feet and handed her the wrench,

taking care that their fingers didn't so much as even brush against each other in the exchange.

She felt a lump form in the back of her throat and tightened her grip on the wrench.

"I called my informant a little while ago," he said, glancing down at the ground and crossing his arms against his chest. "He's got most of the info together. I'm thinking another two days, three at the outside, before the story breaks and we can head on back."

She moved closer to the generator. He immediately stepped aside as though he couldn't bear to stand an inch closer to her than he absolutely had to.

"So soon?" she asked. "I thought it would take at least a week to get the story published."

"Yeah, well, I suggested he make it his top priority. Suggested rather strongly, in fact."

"I see." She swallowed hard and opened the metal covering to the generator. "You know, darling," she said, trying to keep her tone light and casual. "If I didn't know better, I might be persuaded into thinking that you bullied him into moving faster because you couldn't wait to get rid of me."

He flushed. "It's not that."

"Oh, no?"

She gave the inner workings of the generator a quick once-over but didn't find anything obviously out of place. She glanced back at Jake.

"Then if I were to ask you right now to go back

inside the cabin and make love to me again, would you say yes?"

She tried to keep her tone as casual as before, but she was afraid she wasn't succeeding very well.

"If I were to suggest that we forget all about the damn story," she went on, "forget about your informant, about Todd, about everything, and just stay here at Lou's cabin forever, loving each other, would you say yes . . . or would you say no?"

She held her breath, waiting for Jake's answer. She knew that he still wanted her. The hunger, the all-consuming need, still burned as brightly as ever in his eyes, although there was a far darker emotion in them just then that seemed to overshadow his desire for her.

"As . . . pleasurable . . . as I know that would be for us both," he said, his voice filled with regret, "I'm afraid I'd have to say no."

"Do I get to ask why?"

She turned back to the generator and opened the fuel cap to check the level of gasoline, not sure if she could even look at him.

"You already know why," he told her. "We're just not right for each other. Our backgrounds, our lives, they're just too diverse for a relationship to ever work. Hell, your father probably spends more on tuxedos and fancy limos in a single month than I make working at the *Sentinel* in an entire year."

She felt her cheeks begin to flame. "Do you really think I'm so shallow that I could care about how much money you do or don't make?"

"Well, no, but—I mean, you're an heiress. You're used to the best life can offer. Me, I'm just a reporter working for a glorified tabloid. Even if I change jobs after the story breaks, my annual income will still be a lot less than what you're used to."

"Jake, you're being ridiculous again."

"Am I? The point is, people like you and me, we just can't mix for too long without money becoming an issue. Hell, we even got into a fight at the Real McCoy's over a pair of silk pajamas that weren't in our budget."

"That's not fair. We needed something to sleep in, and I was more than willing to compromise with the flannel. Dammit, Jake, you're not even giving us a chance!"

Something told her he never would.

He scowled. "Look, yesterday you told me you thought our stay at the cabin could become some great romantic adventure. And you were right. It did. But the problem with romantic adventures, Maggie darlin', is the same problem with all fantasies: Sooner or later reality has to come crashing in and end them."

His gaze bored into her. "And the reality here is that last night was a mistake—a mistake that neither one of us can afford to repeat."

She stared at him for a moment, knowing it was pointless to argue with him, because he'd already made up his mind about them long before, and nothing she could ever say now would likely change his mind.

"Fine," she said. "It's over. But just answer me one question, Jake."

She knew her voice sounded soft and steeped in emotion, but she couldn't help herself, even though a part of her hated her vulnerability where he was concerned, hated even more the way she couldn't stop wanting a man who'd made it so clear that he just didn't want her.

"Is it me personally that you find so distasteful?" She twisted the fuel cap closed again. "Or is it some ghost woman from your past that you should have laid to rest a long time ago?"

He stiffened but didn't answer her.

She tossed the wrench to the ground at his feet. "The generator's fine," she said. "But like our relationship . . . I guess it just ran out of gas before it ever got started."

She turned and walked back into the cabin.

There was an old adage Jake remembered seeing on a poster in college, something about the road to hell being paved with good intentions. He'd always found it amusing, but by ten the next morning, while Maggie was taking a long walk through the woods and he was pacing through the small cabin like some lovesick fool, Jake was convinced he was a living testament to the validity of the saying.

All he had wanted to do was save them both from themselves. All he'd succeeded in doing, however, was tearing them both apart, one tiny sliver of their souls at a time.

He wanted Maggie, needed her—hell, he loved her—far more now, after he'd tried to assure both himself and her that they couldn't possibly have a future together, than he had before.

Having to share the cabin with her, having to pass close enough to her that he couldn't help but inhale the soft scent of her freshly shampooed hair, yet not passing close enough to quite touch her, hurt more than he could have possibly imagined.

Having to sit across from her at the table for meals or the occasional card game, sitting close enough for him to see the pain shadowing her hazel eyes but not being able to do a damn thing to make it better, hurt even more.

Having to sleep in the same room with her, separated only by a thin blanket—one that *she'd* draped across the cord this time—being haunted by the memories of holding her slender body in his arms while she slept, of the sweet taste of her mouth and sensuous caress of her tongue moving against his when they kissed, of the satiny feel of her skin beneath his fingers, being constantly reminded of all these things but being too much of a damned coward to tell her that he was wrong was slowly killing him.

Maggie was nothing like Alyssa, and it wasn't fair to either him or to Maggie to let his fear of being hurt keep them apart. And after wearing off a good inch or two of the cabin's hardwood floor, he decided it was time he did something about it.

So he left the cabin and went after her.

Jake finally caught up with Maggie about fifteen minutes later.

She was sitting on a large rock next to a mountain stream. She'd drawn up her knees to her chin and wrapped her arms around her calves. Her sunbathed golden hair tumbled freely down her back and shoulders, making her look as innocent and guileless as a child, yet still as beautiful and seductive as a woman—a woman he longed to hold in his arms again, regardless of the emotional cost.

She hadn't noticed his arrival yet. She was tossing pine needles and bits of grass into the slow-moving stream that ran through the stand of old-growth pines at the edge of the clearing. It seemed as though her thoughts were light-years away from the mountains, light-years away from him.

"Is it safe to join you?" he asked, taking a step closer to her.

She glanced over her shoulder to meet his gaze. The trace of a smile hovered around her lips.

"Afraid I'll push you into the creek if you get too close to me, Mr. Wilder?"

He smiled back. "The thought did occur to me . . . Ms. Thorpe."

"Guilty conscience?"

"A little," he said, moving closer. "And I've got a strong hunch that you're still angry with me."

Her smile slowly faded. "But I was never angry with you, Jake."

Her soft voice was shaded with a bittersweet roughness that wrapped itself completely around his soul.

"A little frustrated with you, perhaps," she said. She dropped the last of the pine needles into the stream and dusted off her hands. "A little disappointed maybe. But not angry."

She slid off the rock as he came even with it.

Mere inches separated them, although it felt to him like miles, so many miles that it might take him a lifetime to bridge them all.

"And a little hurt too?" he asked softly.

He raised his hand and stroked her cheek. Her skin felt just as soft and supple as he remembered. His abdominal muscles began to tighten.

"Maybe," she said, her voice dropping to almost a whisper.

"I'm sorry, Maggie."

He slid his fingers slowly down her cheek to stroke her chin, amazed that he could derive so much pleasure from such a simple act as touching her face.

"I swear I never meant that to happen," he said.

"It's . . . okay," she said, pushing his hand away. "You tried to warn me that you weren't interested in anything long-term. I should have listened to you. If I got hurt, I have no one to blame but myself."

"But it's not okay. All those things I said about our lives being too diverse, about how your money would eventually come between us . . . they were just an excuse. Because you were right. This—it's not about you. None of it has been about you or about us."

Her gaze locked with his. "Then whom has it been about?" she asked softly. "Who burned you so bad that you flinch at the sight of fire? Some lover from a remembered past life? Your first crush in kindergarten? Who?"

He sighed. "Try an ex-wife. Her daddy owns Pembrooke Oil, and *they* produce most of the petroleum-based products in the southern U.S. Old man Pembrooke may not have the bucks and political savvy of your daddy, Maggie darlin', but he was still rich enough to make Alyssa a pampered little debutante, and she wore it like a badge of honor."

Maggie's gaze remained locked with his, but she didn't say anything.

"About five years ago I was working for the *Atlanta Constitution*," he went on. "And I was a regular hotshot reporter too. Some even said I was on the fast track for a Pulitzer, and then I met Alyssa. I thought I loved her, that she was everything I'd ever wanted all rolled up into one beautiful package. I was wrong."

"So what happened?" she asked.

He shrugged. "A lot of little things. Maybe I

spent too much time pursuing a story, not enough time at home with her. I admit my priorities were a little skewed back then. It's a mistake I promised myself that I wouldn't make again, not that it would have mattered much with Alyssa. We just weren't very compatible in the first place."

He raked his fingers through his hair. "As for what caused the final breakup, hell, I don't know. Maybe she got tired of playing the happy homemaker, tired of family dinners at my parents' with all my nieces and nephews. Tired of me. Whatever it was, she decided to leave me shortly before our first wedding anniversary for a man whose social prospects and bank account looked a lot more attractive to her than mine obviously did."

He drew a deep breath and crossed his arms against his chest.

"I was working on a big story about the time Alyssa told me she wanted a divorce. The breakup hit me hard. Wounded my pride mostly. I guess I kind of lost it for a while there, and I pushed for publication on the exposé before I could prove it."

"I remember reading about it," she said softly. "Your source disappeared, and the paper was hit with a nasty lawsuit."

He nodded. "After the scandal broke I was treated like a pariah by the mainstream news media. I was damn lucky the *Sentinel* agreed to hire me . . . and even luckier that Lou trusts me enough to give me the journalistic freedom that he does."

"So now you don't print stories that you can't back up with hard evidence," she said.

"Exactly."

She looked him square in the eye. "And you don't fall in love with heiresses either."

He held her gaze for a moment. "Until I met you, no, I didn't. But now . . ."

He slid his hands around her waist and pulled her closer until their bodies touched, until the heat rising off her slender frame burned through his clothes, making him shiver, making him feel as though his bones and muscles and sinew would all melt from its intense warmth, along with the last of his doubts about letting himself love her.

"Now I'm beginning to see just how stupid having such a hard and fast rule can be," he said.

She gave him another smile, a much warmer smile this time. It was more like the kind she used to give him before he'd tried to shatter her heart into a million pieces.

"Some rules can be really stupid, can't they?" she murmured.

She ran her hands up his chest. The warmth of her fingers reached through his chambray shirt to scorch his skin. His body tightened, grew hard.

"Incredibly stupid," he murmured back. "Because I need you, Maggie darlin'."

He pressed his lips against the side of her neck, then her chin, moving steadily closer to her mouth.

"I need your love," he whispered. "Since the moment I met you, you've been all I can think about, all I can dream about. Sometimes I think I've just lost my mind from wanting you so much . . . other times, I think the insanity must come from thinking that I can let you walk away from me. Because I can't. Not now. Probably not ever."

His lips brushed over hers, lightly at first. He half expected her to shove him away and knew he really couldn't blame her if she did. Instead, she gave a long sigh and melted against him, winding her arms around his back to pull him closer. Then she gently thrust her tongue into his mouth to return his kiss with a passion that shook his very soul.

Sometime later, he slowly pulled back to look at her. Her gaze was streaked with passion, tempered with love. He felt himself tremble from its power.

"Maggie, I—"

"Shh," she murmured. "No more words."

Her lips slid over his again, and she pulled him down to the bed of soft pine needles on the ground.

NINE

Jake said he still wanted her.

Maggie's heart thudded wildly as she pressed herself closer to him, gliding her hands along his face, his neck, smoothing her palms over the tightly corded muscles of his shoulders and back, needing to stroke him, needing to touch as much of him as she possibly could and damning the clothes that frustrated her efforts by keeping her from his bare skin.

She felt gripped by a passion unlike any she'd ever felt before, seized by a flame hotter than any fire she'd ever known. Wanting to return the pleasure that his confession had given her, she let her kisses become more frenzied, more urgent. She rubbed her tongue against his, teasing him, gently sucking on his tongue until she heard him softly moan, until she felt him weave his fingers through her hair to pull her closer.

He still wanted her, she thought jubilantly, massaging his shoulders, feeling his muscles tense and shudder beneath her fingertips.

He still needed her.

He'd said that he'd never again put his career before a relationship as though he'd somehow realized that had once been her greatest fear. Now, however, knowing that she'd always have to compete with his career didn't seem to bother her as much as it once had. Probably because now she knew that having only part of Jake's attention was preferable to having none of it.

Maggie moved closer.

He said he still wanted her. That he'd dreamed about her since the moment they'd met. Said, too, that he couldn't give her up—not now, possibly not ever.

He'd said all those wonderful things to her and more, but he hadn't said the one thing she'd wanted most to hear him say.

He hadn't said he loved her.

In fact, he'd danced around the issue as skillfully as Fred Astaire did around Ginger Rogers in one of those old Hollywood musicals.

Yet Maggie knew that Jake cared for her. She could feel the emotional surrender in his lips when he kissed her, offering her his body and his heart and even his soul, holding nothing back, giving her his all, just as she'd hoped that he would.

His hands slid up her sides, skimming over the fabric of her blue plaid chambray shirt to cup her breasts, sending fire-laden tremors leaping through her from the caress of his palms.

He slowly rubbed his thumbs across her nipples until they tightened and throbbed against the fabric of her bra, aching for the damp feel of his tongue against them, aching for the caress of his too-skillful hands against her fevered flesh.

Then he deepened their kiss, seducing her with the sinfully erotic massage of his tongue against hers, arousing her with his touch until she ached to have him thrust himself into her, moving hot and deep and hard, filling her with his love until their bodies finally shuddered in a mutually explosive release.

"Oh, Jake . . ."

She clutched at his shoulder, trying to communicate the hunger she had for him but knowing that mere words could never describe what she felt.

He pressed his fingertips into her hips, searing through the coarse fabric of her jeans like a blast from a furnace through a piece of cellophane. Then he lifted her hips until she could straddle him, until his arousal could rest hard and strong against her groin.

Her mouth went dry. Her heart began to pound. A jolt of unadulterated longing, of pure desire, shook her until she trembled.

"Amazing how we seem to operate under only two speeds, isn't it?" he murmured huskily.

She moaned something that sounded incoherent even to her own ears and started to move against him.

What was amazing to her was that as close as they were—so close that she could swear she felt his heart thudding against the walls of his chest, hear the rush of blood racing through his veins—it wasn't nearly close enough to satisfy her yearning for him.

He nuzzled her neck, bombarding her emotional defenses with dozens of soft, featherlike kisses and sensually charged flicks of his tongue against her skin, then brushing his beard-rough cheek against her until she shivered, certain she was spiraling headlong into an internal meltdown that she seemed powerless to stop.

"We either go full throttle or full stop," he whispered against her ear.

Then he rocked her against him over and over and over again until liquid heat began to pool in her lower abdomen, setting her soul aflame with a fire that could never be cooled.

She gasped as a spasm gripped her. This was too intense, she thought, shuddering against him. It felt much too damned good to ever last.

"It's like there's no in-between for us," he said. "No neutral or idle. No second or third gears. Only an everything-all-at-once or a nothing-at-all."

"I . . . know," she whispered back.

She kissed his neck, the curve of his ear, his beard-stubbled cheek, which he still hadn't shaved,

every part of him that her mouth could reach.
Then she moved her hips in slow rhythm with his,
feeling him grow harder beneath her, wanting
more than anything to feel that hardness locked
deep inside her.

"Of . . . the . . . two speeds," she said,
struggling to maintain her control. "I have to say I
prefer the full throttle to the full stop, because
when you stop, Jake, it nearly kills me."

Keeping her hips pressed against his, he raised
himself up to brush her damp hair from her forehead. His gaze held hers for several moments. His
expression was hard, intense. She felt her abdominal muscles begin to constrict.

"It kills me too, sweetheart," he murmured.

"Then don't fight this anymore," she said.
"Don't be afraid of what you feel for me. Just go
with it, darling. Everything will be wonderful. I
promise."

Though which one of them she was trying to
reassure most, she really couldn't say. She knew she
was still taking a gamble with her heart, one that
might end up costing her far more than she was
willing to pay. All Jake had really told her was that
he wanted her, needed her, maybe even cared a
little bit about her. He hadn't said he thought they
could have a future together. And until he did, she
would still be playing an everything-all-at-once or
nothing-at-all game with him and praying that the
odds were in her favor.

Jake drew a slow breath, held it for a moment,

then exhaled, sliding his hands down her arms, making her skin tingle and burn beneath her long-sleeved shirt.

"But I want—I *need*—more than just a few hours making love with you out here in the woods, Maggie darlin'," he said.

She leaned up to touch his face, stroking his eyebrows with her thumbs, smoothing out the worry lines on his forehead with her fingertips.

"Do you want forever?" she asked.

She knew her voice was betraying far too much of her soul, but she was too swept up in the moment to fear for her own self-preservation.

"Is that what you're trying to tell me, Jake?"

He groaned, then gently rolled her off him until she lay against the ground. She was dimly aware of the nearby gurgling creek, of the breeze rustling the branches of the trees, sending the fragrant scent of pine drifting around her.

Her heart began to pound even faster than before. Her gaze locked with his. And she waited for his answer.

"Forever wouldn't be nearly long enough for me," he said.

His voice was as rough with emotion, as ragged with desire, as hers had been.

"There's so much I want to tell you," he said, rubbing his thumb along her cheek. "So many things that I know I need to say, things about you, about us. I still can't make you any promises, Maggie. I know what you want from me, and I wish to God that I could—"

"Shh . . ."

She was afraid to let him continue. Afraid of what he might say.

"No more words, remember?" she murmured.

She fumbled with the buttons on his shirt, needing to touch him, to hold his body against her, to feel him inside her. Needing the reassurance of his passion then more than she did another breath . . . needing to take one final gamble on their love.

Everything-all-at-once, or nothing-at-all.

"Right now," she said, undoing the last button and pushing his shirt aside, "I think we should let our hearts do the talking."

She touched him, feeling his soft chest hair rustle beneath her fingers. The heat of his body seeped through her palms, firing her blood.

"Right . . . now . . ." she whispered, "I think we need to let our bodies communicate everything that needs to be said between us."

He gave her a smile. "Maybe you're right."

He kissed her, framing her face with his hands, sliding his tongue into her mouth with well-practiced ease to seek out her own, kissing her with a tenderness that threatened to make her come undone.

She helped him shrug off his shirt, then she ran her hands down his chest, loving its heat, its masculine hardness, needing him so much that her hands began to shake. She fumbled with the zipper on his blue jeans, trying to tug it down, but it wouldn't budge.

He chuckled softly. "Because I like the way your body communicates with mine," he said, gently pushing her hand away to undo his zipper.

He pried off his sneakers, then pulled down his jeans and kicked them aside, leaving on only his white cotton boxers. The outline of his arousal strained against the fabric of his shorts, making her breath catch in her throat. Her abdominal muscles constricted again.

"And I like the way your body feels too," he added, his voice strained now.

He tugged her chambray shirt out of her jeans and started to undo the buttons, moving as quickly as she had done with him. Each brush of his fingertips through the ever-widening opening of her top was like another splash of gasoline tossed onto a fire that was already raging too far out of control.

She shivered from its heat, shivered from its power, shivered from the want of him that seemed to spin tighter and tighter inside her.

"I like its curves and its softness," he said, helping her take off her shirt. He lovingly stroked her abdomen, then slid his fingers up to grasp the lace edges of her brassiere.

"I like the way you smell," he went on. "Of roses . . . and of woman . . . your scent drugs me. And I like the way you taste when your body falls apart. So sweet . . . so good."

She felt herself flush and squeezed her eyes closed. Another shudder racked her body.

"I like how your body hugs mine," he added hoarsely, sliding his hands around her back to loosen the clasp on her bra. "And the way you make me feel when I fall apart inside you . . . like I've finally come home."

"But you are home, darling," she whispered, opening her eyes to meet his gaze. "With me you'll always be home. Always."

Her fingers trembled as she undid her jeans and tried to pull them off. He grasped the waistband and helped her. She pried off her sneakers and tugged down her jeans.

"Jake, I . . ."

"Shh," he said, easing her panties off, gliding his hand between her legs to touch her. "No more words, remember?"

He guided a finger inside her wetness, stretching the walls of her body, sending wave after wave of pleasure ricocheting through her with his touch. She reached for his boxers, but he'd already removed them. She glided her hand around the curve of his hip. The satiny warmth of his rigid shaft pressed hard against her thighs. She shuddered again and moved her legs apart, urging him closer.

"No more words," she whispered back.

Their passion would say all that needed to be said.

Then she opened for him, and he slid into her

welcoming heat with a moan that seemed torn from somewhere deep inside him. Their rhythm was fast and furious, then slow and deliberate, alternately gloriously pagan and unbearably tender. And when the fireburst built inside them both to the point of explosion, taking them to the precipice of their desire and beyond, she hugged him with her body, tightening her grip on his soul, hoping that she was bringing him home to her forever.

Time became precious to Maggie, precious because she didn't know how much of it she and Jake would have together at the cabin before his article was published and they had to return to Los Angeles. So, rather than concentrate on how few hours they might have left, she tried to make the most of the time they had been given, making each moment together count.

They took long, leisurely walks through the mountains, linked arm in arm, and they talked for hours curled up on the lumpy bed back in the cabin with her head resting against his chest, hearing the steady, reassuring beat of his heart in her ear, feeling his arm locked tightly around her shoulder.

She told him about growing up in San Francisco, about the sometime loneliness of being an only child and about how ignored she'd often felt by her father's frequent absences because of his obsession with his political campaigns and the family business. She talked about how, to compensate for her loneliness, she'd brought home so many stray pets to her parents' estate, from cats and dogs to snakes and birds, that they'd accused her of trying to open her own private zoo, although they never made her give up a single one. She even confessed to him how she'd always wanted to find some deserted island in the Pacific and run naked through the surf at dawn so she could tell her future grandkids about it one day.

Jake told her about growing up in rural Georgia with his schoolteacher parents, a bossy older brother, and two even bossier younger sisters, who were all married now with kids of their own. He talked about how he'd started a weekly newspaper when he was eight, how he'd done his first exposé on price gouging of candy bars at the local elementary school in its premiere issue, knowing even then what he wanted to do with his life. He told her how he'd always wanted to sail a boat off to some exotic port, although he still didn't know his aft from his bow, and that maybe, one day, he would sail them both to her island, where they could both run through the surf at dawn.

For the next three days, they talked and laughed and talked some more, sharing secrets that they'd never told to another living soul, discussing both the important and the inconsequential of their lives with equal enthusiasm, equal deference.

And when they grew tired of sharing words, they let their bodies communicate their thoughts, spending hours touching . . . caressing . . . kissing.

Loving.

It was her romantic fantasy brought to startling reality, a reality made all the more poignant because she didn't know how long it might last.

For now she had Jake. She had his love, had his heart.

Which—for now—was all that really mattered.

At a few minutes past seven on Wednesday morning, their sixth day at the cabin, Jake stood at the antique kitchen sink, smoothing a handful of lather over his cheeks and neck. He leaned down and checked his reflection in the battered cookie sheet that he'd propped against the wall behind the sink, turning his chin first one way, then the other, trying to find the best place to start his shave. The cookie sheet wasn't offering much in the way of help, but it was the closest thing the cabin had to a mirror.

He rinsed his hands in the pan of warm water that he'd put in the sink, then reached for one of Maggie's disposable pink razors just as she strolled into the kitchen, stifling a yawn.

"Oh, be still my heart."

Her low, husky voice was playfully seductive, warming him from the inside out.

"Don't tell me you've finally decided to shave that awful thing off," she teased.

He grinned and glanced at her.

Her hair was tumbling around her shoulders in sleep-tossed disarray, and she was flashing him that much-too-naughty smile of hers. Her feet were bare, and she'd slipped into the red and black checked pajama top. Even though the flannel top was oversized and its open collar fell just short of her cleavage, he still felt it was far sexier than any skimpy satin and lace nightie, simply because Maggie was wearing it.

She was beautiful, he thought, feeling a rush of emotion wash over him.

Absolutely breathtaking.

When she came even with the sink, he pulled her to him for a brief hug, loving the way she felt in his arms. She still smelled of him and of feminine softness, of home and hearth and of all things wonderful.

He gave her a kiss on her nose, depositing a smear of shaving cream on her chin in the process.

"Don't act so surprised, darlin'," he said. "We both know you nagged me into it. First by leaving the razor and the can of shaving cream out on the kitchen table so that I couldn't help but notice it when I awoke this morning, then by teasing me with all those comments last night about how my scruffy mountain-man look was beginning to lose its charm. What choice did I have *but* to shave?"

She grinned, then dabbed at the lather on her chin and dunked her finger in the pan of water in the sink to swish it around.

"Sorry, darling," she said, "but it was becoming a matter of self-preservation. You were giving me whisker burns on parts of my anatomy that were . . . well, ultrasensitive."

He felt himself flush. His body began to tighten, grow hard.

"Besides, I love the way you look when you're clean-shaven," she went on. "I love looking at that adorable dimple in your chin. I love kissing it, and I can't really do that when you've got a beard, now, can I?"

"It's not a dimple," he reminded her. "It's a cleft."

"It's a dimple, Jake, and I love the way it winks at me when you smile."

She slid her arms around his waist and hugged him again. "So please hurry up and shave," she said, sounding breathless. "The anticipation of kissing you again is practically overwhelming me."

His abdominal muscles constricted. His heart started to pound. He laughed, feeling fairly over-whelmed himself, and gently pushed her away.

"I'm trying, believe me," he said. "But without a decent mirror I can't see what I'm doing . . . and having you distract me like this doesn't help much either."

He leaned down to check his reflection in the cookie sheet again and lifted the razor.

"Then why don't you let me do it for you?" she suggested softly. "Just like those hardy pioneer women used to do for their men back in early California."

She reached for the razor. Her fingers brushed against his, sending electric shivers shuddering down his spine.

"I'm not really up on all my California history, darlin'," he murmured, "but I don't think pioneer women used to shave their men. And even if they did, they wouldn't have used a hot-pink disposable razor."

"So we improvise, which is the true essence of a hardy pioneer spirit, don't you think?"

She grinned and hopped onto the counter. The bottom of her pajama top started to slide up her thighs, giving him an even better view of her long, tanned legs. She tugged on the waistband of his jeans and pulled him closer until his hips rested against her body.

"Now, relax, darling," she said, "and let me take care of everything."

He chuckled softly, gliding his hands up her legs, luxuriating in the feel of her warm, smooth skin beneath his palms.

"Relaxing . . . may . . . be a little difficult just now," he said huskily. "You feel too good . . . look too damned luscious."

He moved his hands under her top to stroke the curve of her hips, feeling the heat of her body scorch through his fingertips and fire his blood.

"Maybe we should try shaving me a little later," he murmured. "Say after we've made love for another hour . . . or another decade. Maybe a century or two."

Her grin deepened. She slapped at his hands. "Behave yourself, Jake Wilder, before I accidentally nick a major artery or something."

She tilted his chin up with the tip of her index finger. He sighed and closed his eyes, giving in. Moments later he felt her press the edge of the razor close to the bottom of his neck and slowly pull it upward, gently scraping along his skin in one smooth stroke. She rinsed the razor in the pan of water, tapped it once against the side of the pan, then repeated the process.

"Not bad," he murmured when the second swipe was complete, still keeping his eyes closed. "And I didn't even feel a single nick."

She tilted his neck in the opposite direction and continued to shave him.

"Pretty amazing, huh?" she murmured. "Especially since I've never done this before."

What was amazing, he thought as she cut a swath through the lather along his neck, was how the feel of her hand against his skin could still send his heart racing out of control, as though each time she touched him were the very first.

"*Now* you tell me that you've never shaved a man before," he said, feigning concern. "When you've got me at your mercy . . . when my neck is literally on the chopping block."

She drew another long swath across his neck, following it with several shorter strokes.

"Yes, but, if I'd told you that I hadn't done this before, you'd have probably turned my offer down flat," she said.

She moved on to his face now, gliding the razor from his cheeks down to his jawline in short, measured strokes, then concentrating her attention on his chin, using such care, it made him feel as though he were the most precious thing in the world to her.

"And I did so want to shave you, darling," she murmured.

He leaned into her, wishing it could last forever. Wishing that he could stand there in the kitchen, having her shave him well into infinity itself. He loved the feel of her hands moving along his face, loved the way he felt so dependent upon her, loved the intimacy of their act.

He loved her.

"Did you really hate my beard that much?" he asked.

"Well, yes, but that's not why I wanted to shave you."

"Then why?"

She turned his face again and started to shave the other side.

"Because I love having you at my mercy," she teased. "I love knowing that you trust me with your neck and your face and even your adorable dimple, and—you do trust me, don't you, darling?"

He opened his eyes and met her gaze.

"Implicitly," he murmured. "Without hesitation."

She lowered the razor and swished it through the pan of water. "Enough to let me do this every day?"

She shaved above his upper lip, manipulating the razor ever so carefully over his skin.

"If . . . you'd like," he said softly.

She smiled. "Even when we have to leave the cabin and return to Los Angeles? Will you still let me shave you then?"

He knew what she was doing, asking him without really asking him if they had a future, if they would still be together when they returned to Los Angeles.

She was asking him questions he still didn't know if he could answer yet.

He took the razor from her hand and dropped it into the sink next to the pan of water.

"Who says we ever have to go back?" he murmured hoarsely.

Then he slid his arms around her waist and drew her close to him, seeking out her mouth in a fiercely possessive kiss, vowing never to let her go.

The sharp trill of his cellular telephone awoke Jake two hours later.

Muttering a curse under his breath, he raised himself up and grabbed the phone from the top of the dresser. Then he punched the button to activate the receiver and slumped back on the bed just as Maggie began to stir beside him.

"Jake Wilder," he said in a semi-grumble.

"Congratulate yourself," Lou said, sounding unbearably jovial. "You've just scored the scoop of the year."

Jake went immediately still. His body. His heart. Everything inside him seemed to freeze.

He swallowed hard. "So my source came through?" he asked.

"Big-time," Lou said. "In addition to the receipts and credit vouchers, he sent us a copy of one of Vedder's internal memos which spell out the deal he struck with Kingfisher over that senatorial vote-buying business. Regardless of what happens on election day, McNichols's political career is finished."

"Is that Lou?" Maggie murmured, snuggling closer and winding her arm around his waist.

Jake nodded. As always, her touch, her nearness, sent a comforting warmth sluicing through his veins, although this time it wasn't enough to dissolve the tight knot forming in the pit of his stomach.

It was too soon, he thought, feeling a wave of panic wash over him. He needed more time alone with her. If not another week, then another day, or at least a few more hours.

Seemingly oblivious of his inner turmoil, she flashed him a smile, then pulled the receiver down so they could share it.

"Hi, Lou," she said. "When's Jake's article coming out?"

"It was the lead story in this morning's edition," Lou told her. "The paper is flying off the newsstands too. The wire services have already picked it up, and most of the local TV stations opened with the story as their top news item. Hell, this thing's even gone international. I got a call from your parents about an hour ago, Maggie, who said they'd heard the news over Brazilian radio when their boat docked for supplies. They're already in flight and should be in Los Angeles early this afternoon."

"What about Todd?" she asked. "Has he said anything about it?"

"Not yet. But he's scheduled a press conference for noon at the Universal Hilton. I know it's short notice, but I was hoping you two could make it."

Jake tightened his hold on her. "I, ah, don't know if that's feasible," he said. "It's about a two-hour drive back into the city, and with the traffic this time of day . . ."

"Oh, don't be silly," Maggie said. She leaned over him to check the time on the travel alarm clock sitting on top of the dresser. "Why, it's only about nine-thirty now. If we hurry, we should just about make it."

She slipped out of his arms before he could stop her and scrambled out of bed to get dressed.

"Great," Lou said. "Then it's settled."

"But it's not—"

The phone went dead.

". . . settled," Jake finished with a sigh of frustration.

It looked as though his time in which to settle things between him and Maggie had just run out.

TEN

. . . The problem with romantic adventures, Maggie darlin', is the same problem with all fantasies: Sooner or later reality has to come crashing in and end them.

Holding on to Jake's hand so tightly that her fingers were going numb, Maggie cast a worried glance at him out of the corner of her eye as they weaved their way through the throng of reporters staking out their territory in the grand ballroom of the Universal Hilton.

Jake's words had haunted her all during the long, tense drive down from the San Bernardino Mountains. His words had played over and over in her head while he sat quiet and still beside her, keeping his eyes focused on the traffic, his continued silence making her feel as if he'd already shut her out of his life . . . and out of his heart.

More than anything, she wished she could drag him off to some secluded corner of the hotel so she could run her fingers lovingly through his tousled hair and ask him to talk to her about what he was feeling. She wished it with every cell of her body, but she knew that she'd never have the courage to do it.

How could she, when she was too afraid of what he might tell her? After all, this was his big moment. His story had finally broken, the one that would put him back on the top as an investigative journalist. The press conference was about to begin—where his excruciatingly researched exposé would likely be discussed in minute detail, making him the man of the hour—yet Jake looked tight-lipped and troubled, as though he wished that he could be anywhere other than the hotel just then.

Or maybe, she thought, feeling a wave of sadness wash over her, he just wished that he could be anywhere other than with her. As much as she didn't want to admit the truth, she knew that their romantic adventure was slowly reaching its end. And he still hadn't said a single word about their future, or even if he thought they could have one.

"I was beginning to think you two weren't going to make it," Lou murmured, coming alongside them.

"Yeah, well, we're here now," Jake said, sounding none too pleased by the fact. "So why don't we take our seats before somebody spots Maggie and this thing turns into an even bigger circus."

Reaching up with her free hand to tug down on the rim of her cowboy hat, Maggie took a quick look around the room. Jake's fears seemed ground-less. The other reporters appeared to be far too interested in running a final diagnostics check on their equipment and on watching the podium for Todd's arrival to notice her or anything else.

Not that she imagined it would matter all that much even if they *did* recognize her. With Jake's story already out, she had no more reason to hide from Todd's goons. She had no more reason to stay with Jake. . . .

Lou motioned toward three chairs he'd reserved at the back of the room, and they headed toward them.

Jake slid into the middle seat, releasing her hand. Maggie sat next to him, fighting hard against the urge to cry.

Seconds later a large murmur went through the room, followed by the click and flash of cameras as a pale and noticeably nervous Todd strode into the ballroom. He was surrounded by several members of his staff, although his campaign manager, Ray-mond Kingfisher, was nowhere to be seen.

Todd approached the podium and cleared his throat. Then, without further preamble, he un-folded a couple of pieces of paper and started to read from them.

His statement was brief, not more than five minutes in length, and movingly heartfelt, filled with references to "his dedicated staff" and the "errors in judgment" they'd made on his behalf.

Surprisingly though—at least it was to Maggie—Todd admitted that some of Jake's allegations were correct. The timber industry had funded several of Todd's excursions to the Caribbean, for which he was now deeply sorry; a check was being messengered to Vedder's Washington, D.C., office that day in full reimbursement.

While Todd was quick to deny that he had ever sold his senatorial votes to Karl Vedder or anyone else, he also admitted that Raymond Kingfisher had confessed to entering into improper discussions with Vedder about Todd's position on certain pieces of future legislation that would affect the timber industry.

After advising that Raymond Kingfisher had since tendered his resignation—and would be issuing his own statement later that day—Todd refolded the sheets of paper and turned to leave the ballroom.

His performance, Maggie decided, had been slick, well-rehearsed, and beautifully played. It was so good, in fact, that unless someone did something fairly quick, she was afraid he might pull the whole thing off.

The reporters sprang into action, rushing the podium, pummeling Todd with questions about Jake's allegations, about Todd's plans for his campaign, all of which he calmly ignored.

Todd had almost made it to the exit when Jake slowly rose to his feet.

"Jake Wilder, Senator McNichols. *Los Angeles Sentinel.* Just one question, please."

Heads swirled toward the rear of the room. Todd went rigid.

"Are you aware, Senator," Jake went on, "that Karl Vedder wrote a detailed memo concerning a lunch meeting he had with both you and Raymond Kingfisher in which the subject of your position on future key pieces of legislation was not only *discussed* but *agreed upon*?"

One of Todd's handlers tugged on his arm, trying to pull him toward the door, but Todd shrugged the man off. Todd shot Jake a look of pure venom, then turned and walked stiffly back to the podium.

"I know of no such memorandum, Mr. Wilder," Todd said coldly. "Furthermore, I categorically deny any personal knowledge of Raymond Kingfisher's meetings or secret deals with Karl Vedder."

Lou pulled out a sheaf of papers from his valise, which was sitting on the floor next to his chair, and handed them to Jake, who just smiled.

"The memo of which I speak—and I'm holding a photocopy of it right now, Senator—details a meeting between you, Karl Vedder, and Raymond Kingfisher on the twenty-eighth of June in San Francisco. I also have photographs of all three of you meeting on that same date, if you need some help in jogging your memory."

Todd just glared. Jake's smile turned up another degree or two.

"In light of the memo and the photographs,

Senator," Jake said, "is it *still* your position that you were unaware of secret deals made between your office and Karl Vedder concerning your support of specific pieces of legislation regarding the timber industry?"

"Absolutely."

"And do you also deny that Raymond King-fisher met privately with Karl Vedder in your suite here at the hotel seven days ago, during which they discussed the promises you made to Vedder concerning the squashing of the Landerman bill during the next session of Congress?"

Two spots of color began to stain Todd's cheeks. "Again," he said, "I have no personal knowledge of any secret meetings."

"And do you further deny that Vedder and Kingfisher discussed plans to have my investigation into your activities permanently curtailed?" Jake went on, not backing down, making her so proud of him that she wanted to hug him right there on the spot.

"Or that Maggie Thorpe overheard their conversation," Jake added, "forcing her to go into hiding because she feared for her own life?"

"Feared for her life?"

Todd gave a short laugh and glanced toward the exit again, as though he wished he were barreling his way toward it right that very second.

"I hardly think so," he said.

"So you're denying the allegations, then?"

"Absolutely," Todd spat out. "They're completely without merit."

Todd leaned onto the podium, gripping its sides with his hands. "You know, Mr. Wilder, one would have thought that you'd have learned your lesson in Atlanta four years ago about not making accusations you simply cannot prove. Perhaps another slander suit will drive home the point."

Maggie jumped to her feet. "But it's true! I heard Vedder say that Raymond should arrange for Jake to have an accident of some kind, that he was getting too close to finding out that you'd sold your vote on the Landerman bill. I heard it all, Todd."

Jake's smile turned deadly. "Funny thing is, Senator, I kind of believe her—and I think a lot of other people might just believe her too."

"Like me, for example!"

The last comment came from her father, who stood in the doorway of the ballroom next to her mother, positively glowering at Todd.

Pandemonium reigned for a moment. Reporters turned on Todd, clustering around the podium, hammering him for a response, while others rushed to her father, who was making his way over to the podium.

Jake's hand clamped over her arm. She turned to meet his gaze.

"We need to talk," he said.

Before she could murmur a word of protest, he led her through the rows of chairs and out the service entrance of the ballroom into the back hallway.

He glanced over his shoulder as the door swung closed behind them, didn't see anyone following them, and opened the door to the small linen closet where they'd first met seven days before.

Seven short days, Maggie thought in amazement, that had been jam packed with more emotion, with more love and heartache and joy, than an entire lifetime could ever possibly contain.

He turned on the overhead light, ushered her inside the closet, and closed the door after them.

"You . . . want to talk to me?" she asked, feeling her throat constrict, still afraid of what he might say.

"Yes."

Her heart started to pound. Her stomach felt as if it had dropped to her knees.

"But here?" she asked. "Now? I mean, there's a roomful of reporters out there trying to tear Todd to pieces, and you should be gathering the info for the follow-up on your exposé, not to mention the fact that my parents just arrived and—"

She had to stop to take a breath.

"Here," Jake said, moving closer. His body was tense, his expression determined. "Now. Before this goes any further . . . before you leave."

He stopped in front of her. Their gazes locked.

"Because you *were* planning to leave, weren't you, Maggie darlin'?" he asked. "Maybe fly back to San Francisco with your parents later today?"

She flushed. The thought had occurred to her.

"I—well, I haven't exactly been besieged with requests to stay in Los Angeles, now, have I?"

He skimmed his hands up her arms, sending white-hot shivers tumbling through her.

"No, I guess you haven't," he said quietly.

He sighed and started to massage her shoulders. "I'm sorry, Maggie. For putting you—us—through all this. Will you forgive me?"

"What's to forgive?" she asked, knowing her voice was streaked with emotion. "It's not as if you were dishonest with me or anything. It's not as if you promised me a commitment . . . or a future." He'd been careful to avoid promising her either.

"But I want a commitment," he said softly. "And I want a future with you. I want—"

He took a deep breath. "Aw, hell, Maggie, don't you know what I'm trying to say here?"

She shook her head.

He cupped her face in his hands. Her heart went absolutely still.

"I'm trying to tell you that I love you," he said huskily. "That I don't want you to leave. Not to-day, not tomorrow. *Not ever.*"

Jake waited a moment, staring into her eyes, afraid to move, afraid even to breathe. He was afraid that she might tell him that he had waited too damn long to declare his feelings for her and she was no longer interested. Or, worse, that she'd only been swept up by the romantic trappings of their adventure and had never really loved him at all.

"What did you just say to me?" she asked, incredulous.

She slid her hands over his and gently pulled them off her face.

He swallowed hard.

"I—I said that I don't want you to leave," he murmured. "That I want you to stay with me . . . forever."

Maggie stared at him a moment longer, then her expression began to soften.

"Before that," she said. "There were three little words, something about how you felt toward me." She gave him a smile. "And please say them slowly this time, darling, because I want to savor every sweet syllable."

He started to relax, feeling his apprehension, his uncertainty, vanish the moment he saw the love shining in her eyes.

"Three little words?" he murmured, smiling back. "Hmm . . . could they have been something like *I love you* perhaps?"

She started to grin. "Something precisely like *I love you.*"

She took off the cowboy hat and tossed it onto the metal linen cart at the back of the closet. Her hair tumbled around her shoulders in soft golden waves. She slid her palms up his chest to rest on his shoulders.

"Now, tell me again," she said breathlessly. "And then tell me how you felt when you first saw me . . . and when we first kissed . . . and when you first realized that you loved me. Tell me everything."

He laughed and hugged her to him. "That's a tall order, Maggie darlin'. I could talk for hours about any single one of them. Like the night we first met, for example—in this very closet."

"You were trying to crash Todd's fund-raiser and failing so miserably."

"Actually, I thought I had the situation well under control," he told her. "My plan was to wait in here until the guard lost interest, then I was going to slip back into the ballroom with no one the wiser. It might have worked, too, until you strolled in with that bottle of wine tucked under your arm, flashing me a smile so warm, so downright naughty, it threw my concentration to hell and gone . . . and stole my heart clean away."

He wove his fingers through her hair and tilted her face up toward his until he could look in her eyes.

"Now that I think about it," he said softly, "I probably first fell in love with you that same night when you covered for me with Kingfisher."

"Which time?" she asked. "Here in the closet, or when I kissed you up in Todd's room?"

He felt his body tighten. "A little bit of both, but the kiss certainly clinched things. You set my soul on fire, Maggie darlin' . . . and it's been burning ever since."

She stroked his cheek. "And yet you put up such a valiant struggle about it," she said. "Telling me how we were so incompatible, how things could never work out between us. Lucky for you I never believed you."

His heart started to pound. "Damned lucky," he murmured, brushing his lips over hers and pulling her closer.

Sometime later she gently pushed him away.

"So tell me, Jake Wilder," she said, grinning up at him. "Now that you're a hotshot reporter again, are you planning to leave the *Sentinel* behind for greater glory?"

He shook his head. "Unh-unh. I think I'll stay. At least for a little while longer."

"I'm glad," she said. "Because I think it would break Lou's heart if you left, and he might never agree to let us use his cabin again, which would surely break mine."

Jake chuckled. "Good point." He kissed her forehead. "But no matter where I work," he said softly, "I swear I'll never get so wrapped up in a story that I'll ignore you the way your father once did. You have my word."

"Don't worry, darling. I wouldn't let you get away with it even if you tried."

He hugged her again.

"Now what about you and Pet Haven?" he asked. "Exactly when will they be opening the Los Angeles chapter?"

"Soon, we hope. Maybe early January or February of next year, if we can get the funding together."

"You call that soon? It sounds more like an eternity."

"It's only four to five months, darling."

"Yeah, but I can't wait that long to have you all to myself again. I love you, Maggie."

"And I love you," she murmured back.

He pulled her against him again and smiled. "So what do you suppose my chances would be of convincing you to speed up the timetable on your move?"

Her eyes began to twinkle. "Are we talking just a temporary thing here or something permanent?" she asked.

"Permanent definitely."

"Hmm . . . I don't know."

She linked her hands around his neck and kissed his chin.

"Exactly what kind of incentive are you prepared to offer me?" she teased.

His gaze locked with hers. "How about the rest of our lives?" he asked softly. "Laughing . . . loving . . . fulfilling all those dreams we shared back at the cabin. We could—"

A rap sounded on the closet door.

"Jake? Maggie? Are you two in there? It's Bob Liebowitz."

"And Sandy Brenner," Liebowitz's partner chimed in. "May we come in?"

Jake scowled. "No," he said.

The door slowly opened. Brenner and Liebowitz stuck their heads into the closet, grinning from ear to ear.

"Just one picture," Brenner cajoled, wiggling his camera.

"Maybe a brief statement too," Liebowitz added. "Lou's got us on a tight deadline, otherwise we wouldn't dream of intruding on you two right now."

Maggie laughed and unwound her hands from Jake's neck. "It's fine with me, but you'll have to ask Jake."

"And Jake says no. Look, why the hell are you guys bothering us anyway? The *story* is back there." Jake motioned toward the ballroom.

"Who cares about another political scandal?" Brenner asked. "Besides, we cover the entertainment news, and there's nothing more entertaining than a good love story with a happy ending." He glanced from Jake to Maggie. "There, ah, *is* going to be a happy ending, isn't there?"

"Oh, I certainly hope so," Maggie murmured, trying to look serious.

"What do you mean *hope*?" Liebowitz asked. "Hasn't he asked you to marry him yet?"

She shook her head. "Afraid not. And I've been waiting so patiently too."

"What's the holdup, Wilder?" Brenner demanded. "Ask the woman already."

"Out," Jake said.

"But we haven't gotten our picture yet," Liebowitz protested.

"Out!"

Jake took a threatening step forward; Liebowitz and Brenner beat a hasty retreat back into the hallway.

Jake closed the door—firmly. He'd have locked it, too, if the door had had a lock.

"Aw, come on, Jake," Liebowitz called out, banging on the door. "Is this any way to treat a colleague?"

"Go away," Jake yelled back. Then he grinned and pulled Maggie closer to him.

"They're not going to go away, you know," she said.

"Who cares?" he asked. "We have some things to discuss, you and me. Important things."

He tilted her head up to look at him.

"Now, what do you mean, I hadn't asked you to marry me? I thought we were discussing the future a couple of minutes ago, *our* future."

She flushed. "Yes, but you didn't *technically* propose to me, darling. A woman hates to be so presumptuous about things."

"I—well, will you?" he asked. "Marry me, I mean?"

He could see the answer in her eyes, in the way they went soft and misty. He could see it, too, in her smile, feel it in the way her hands skimmed up his arms.

"Hmm, I don't know. This is so sudden," she said, teasing him a little when they both knew what her answer would be. "Let me think about it."

"Think about it on the way to the justice of the peace," he told her.

"You mean you want to get married *now*? Right this minute?"

"Why not? We could slip out the back of the hotel, drive the Jeep to the airport, and hop a plane to Vegas. We could be married quietly before nightfall, and don't worry about Brenner and Liebowitz. They wouldn't dare follow us."

She laughed. "They're not the ones who concern me. You haven't met my mother yet. She's been planning my wedding since the day I was born. It's sort of been like her hobby. If we don't give in to her plans for a big wedding, she'll never forgive either one of us. Besides, she'll just make us have a second, formal ceremony later."

"Fine," he said. "She can plan the biggest wedding she'd like—later. I don't want to wait one more second than I have to for us to get married, darlin'."

He brushed his lips over hers for another kiss that seemed to last forever, though it still wasn't long enough to suit him.

"Hey, Jake," Liebowitz demanded through the door. "Did you ask her yet? Or are we going to have to come in there and help you out?"

Jake grinned. "Yeah, I asked her," he yelled back.

"And?" Liebowitz and Brenner demanded in unison.

Jake met Maggie's gaze.

"And?" he asked softly.

She wound her arms around his neck. "Yes!"

She said it with a rush of emotion, her voice shaded with love and caring, making it seem as if it were the most beautiful word in the entire language.

"I'll marry you, Jake Wilder," she said. "Today if you like, and then again later, when we have that big formal ceremony."

A loud whoop of excitement went up from outside the closet, but it didn't come close to the level of excitement pounding through Jake's veins.

"Say it again," he said. "Tell me that you'll marry me . . . and make it slower this time, darlin', so I can savor every sweet syllable."

"Yes," she said, pulling him closer. "I'll marry you, Jake Wilder."

His heart filled with so much joy, so much happiness, he thought it might burst.

"I love you, Maggie," he said softly.

"I love you too," she whispered back.

He slid his lips over hers in another kiss, savoring the taste of her mouth beneath his, secure in the knowledge that she was finally, truly his.

THE

Loveswept

EDITORS
ARE HAPPY TO ANNOUNCE
THE THREE WINNERS OF
LOVESWEPT'S TREASURED
TALES III CONTEST!

**THERESA BURCHETT
CHRISTY M. ANDERSON
LESLIE-ANN JONES**

OUR CONGRATULATIONS TO
EACH OF THESE TERRIFIC AND
LOYAL LOVESWEPT FANS. TO
READ THEIR PROFILES, PLEASE
TURN THE PAGE.

AND MANY THANKS TO
EVERYONE WHO ENTERED THE
CONTEST.

Theresa Burchett

Theresa is from Southern California, where she has lived all of her life. She is married and is the proud mother of a son and a daughter. Reading is without question a passion of Theresa's—she usually reads a book a day! She has been reading romance for fifteen years, and says that Loveswept is her favorite series because the stories and characters are always interesting. "Years after reading one of your books I could pick it up and remember the characters. Like old friends, they stay in my thoughts," she says.

Theresa's favorite authors include Tami Hoag, Deborah Smith, Sandra Brown, Billie Green, Kay Hooper, Sandra Chastain, and most of all, Iris Johansen.

Christy M. Anderson

Christy got married recently, the day before she mailed her entry to our Treasured
Tales III Contest, in fact. Just goes to show
that true love can bring good luck as well!
Christy is store manager for a men's clothing store as well as an aspiring writer. In
her spare time, she likes to work out, loves
antiques (especially rings), and of course,
loves to read. Christy says that she has
been reading romance "since my mother
would let me," and her favorite Loveswept
authors are Iris Johansen, Jan Hudson,
and Fayrene Preston.

Leslie-ann Jones

Leslie-ann was excited to hear that she had won because she says she always enters contests, but never wins. She is a native of Trinidad, and migrated to America with her younger sister to join her mother in 1984. Along with reading (she has 1,327 books, 598 of which are Loveswepts!), Leslie-ann loves sports, animals, collecting stamps, and participating in Carnival. She is also a graduate of Coppin State College, where she earned a B.S. in management science with a minor in computer science.

THE EDITORS' CORNER

What do a cunning cat-burglar, a self-starting sister, a determined detective and a witty workaholic have in common? Nothing but the most romantic of troubles, as you'll find out in next month's LOVE-SWEPTs. So join these four intriguing heroines as they journey the bumpy road to happily-ever-after . . . and discover that love does indeed conquer all.

Romance star Fayrene Preston adds her own brand of heat with the next book in the Damaron Dynasty series: LOVESWEPT #778, **THE DAMARON MARK: THE WARRIOR.** Jonah Damaron exudes power like a force of nature, untamable and sensual in a way that awakens every nerve ending in Jolie Lanier's body! But she's playing a dangerous game, taking risks for the sake of honor, keeping secrets that Jonah's smile promises he can uncover with the merest whisper of a touch. As fast-paced as a lover's heartbeat, as white-hot as the heat of a candle flame, Fayrene Preston's novel blends daring intrigue and desperate passions, joining an irresistible hero and an unforgettable heroine in a timeless tango of love.

No one touches the heart and tickles the funny bone all at once like Marcia Evanick in **FAMILY FIRST**, LOVESWEPT #779. James Stonewall Carson doesn't look like a grade-school teacher, with his muscled body and shoulders broad enough to carry the world. But there's no mistaking his dedication to the job—or his manly interest in Emmy Lou McNally. Raising six brothers and sisters leaves her no time for dating, but James's sweet talk and fast moves, along with a little help from matchmaking townfolks, pave the way for a delightful courtship. This top-notch read from award-winner Marcia Evanick reveals how tender passion can burn with sizzling heat.

Excitement ripples **UNDER THE COVERS** in Linda Warren's newest LOVESWEPT, #780. He's never been followed by a woman so downright determined, Simon Faro notes with admiration—and more than a touch of curiosity! Detective Jo O'Neal is outrageously persistent in tracking him, even taking on a sassy charade in hopes he'll lead her to criminals she's long been after. Once he proves he's just a reporter nosing around for a scoop, he must convince her to join forces to smoke out the bad guys and set off some fireworks of their own. Linda Warren's steamy romp is a seriously sexy caper that's undeniably fun.

Surrender to the temptation of **SLOW HANDS**, LOVESWEPT #781, by Debra Dixon. Sam Tucker isn't the kind of man to wait for an invitation, not when his mission is to help Clare McGuire learn the joys of losing control! Convinced Sam wants only to change her, the pretty business exec insists she likes her life just as it is—until his kisses brand her with fiery need that echoes her own hunger. Sparring has never been so sweetly seductive as in this delicious treat from Debra Dixon, who entangles a savvy workaholic with a formerly buttoned-down and bottled-up hero determined to show her how to seize the moment.

Happy reading!

With warmest wishes,

Beth de Guzman   Shauna Summers

Senior Editor   Associate Editor

P.S. Watch for these Bantam women's fiction titles coming in February: Tami Hoag's impressive debut hardcover, NIGHT SINS, revealed her to be a masterful spinner of spine-chilling thrills; now, in **GUILTY AS SIN,** she picks up where she left off, delivering non-stop suspense that brings terror to a whole new, even more frightening level. From Teresa Medeiros, nationally bestselling author of FAIREST

OF THEM ALL, comes **BREATH OF MAGIC,** a bewitching time-travel romance about an enchantress from the 17th century who collides with a future beyond her imagining. Finally Jean Stone's **IVY SECRETS** is the emotionally charged story of three former college roommates brought together by the kidnapping of one of their daughters. Be sure to see next month's LOVESWEPTs for a preview of these exceptional novels. And immediately following this page, preview the Bantam women's fiction titles on sale *now*!

Don't miss these extraordinary books
by your favorite Bantam authors

On sale in January:

LION'S BRIDE
by Iris Johansen

SEE HOW THEY RUN
by Bethany Campbell

SCOUNDREL
by Elizabeth Elliott

LION'S BRIDE

BY

IRIS JOHANSEN

A magical weaver of spellbinding tales, enticing characters, and unforgettable romance, Iris Johansen is a "master among master storytellers."* Now the winner of every major romance award returns with a sizzling new novel of passion, peril, and searing sensuality.

The darkly handsome warrior found her in the hot desert night, the last survivor of a caravan devastated by a brutal attack. But Thea could hardly have found a less likely savior. Brooding, powerful, erotic, the infamous Lord Ware felt no need to rescue a total stranger, but Thea's striking beauty and fighting spirit moved him. So the knight in tarnished armor carried her away to his secret stronghold at Dundragon, where she would become his prisoner, his tormentor, his lover . . . and the one weapon his deadly enemy could use to destroy him.

* *Affaire de Coeur*

"You can set your watch by him," one of the teachers
had said.

That's exactly what the twins did every weekday
afternoon on the playground. The boys were eight
and very handsome. They had dark hair and blue-
gray eyes fringed with black lashes. They wore identical military watches, large and unbreakable.

Each day when the tall old gentleman appeared,
rounding the corner, the boys' eyes glittered with interest. They would look first at their watches, then at
each other. The watches should say 2:07, and if they
did not, the twins adjusted them, because the old man
always appeared at 2:07.

Laura would be grateful to see the old gentleman
round the corner, for that meant recess was almost

half over, and soon she would be back in the warmth of the classroom.

The twins, as usual, clutched the fence rails, ignoring the other children, watching for the man. Their winter jackets and gloves were alike in all but color. As usual, Trace wore blue and Rickie red. The boys were so identical that many people could tell them apart only by this color coding. They seemed even to breathe in unison, their breath rising in synchronized plumes toward the sky.

Their hands tightened on the fence when they saw the man coming. The air was so cold that his ears were red and his usually controlled face looked almost pained. His white muffler was wound around his neck, and his coat collar was turned up. He seemed to exhale smoke as he walked, as if he were an elderly and benign dragon.

Perhaps because of the cold, he walked a bit more swiftly than usual, and Trace frowned, trying to keep count of the man's steps. When the old man passed the boys, he lifted his hat, just barely.

"*Good* afternoon," he said, not looking at them, striding on. "*Good* afternoon."

They saluted stiffly, their eyes following him. "*Good* afternoon," they echoed. "*Good* afternoon."

He kept moving briskly. One of the other children, Janine, ran up to Laura, asking for help in retying her shoe. "Of course," Laura said, putting her hand on the girl's shoulder. But she waited, first, to exchange her usual silent greeting with the old gentleman.

His dark eyes met hers. He raised his gloved hand to his hat. He nodded.

Then a long staccato burst of noise split the winter air, and the side of the old gentleman's face exploded into blood. His remaining eye rolled upward, his shattered jaw fell, as if to cry out, but no sound emerged.

Blood blossomed on his chest like red carnations sprouting in full bloom, and blood spurted from his legs, which danced, sinking beneath him. He lurched like a broken puppet toward the street and fell in a ruined heap. His wounds steamed like little mouths exhaling into the cold.

The children screamed, the teachers on the playground screamed, pedestrians screamed, and one woman with a Lord & Taylor shopping bag sat on the sidewalk, screaming as blood poured down her face.

Laura moved on sheer instinct. She wrestled Janine to the ground before the old gentleman hit the sidewalk, and she held her there, her body thrown over the girl's. *Shooting*, Laura thought in horror, ducking her head, *somebody's shooting at us.*

A bullet richocheted shrilly off the pavement of the playground, and one of the children—William, perhaps?—screamed even more loudly.

Her face hidden, she heard Herschel's agonized cry. "He's hit! He's hit!"

Then the shooting stopped and she heard the squeal of tires. Without the shots, the air seemed to ring with silence—except for the screams, of course, but they hardly registered on Laura's consciousness any longer.

"He's hit! He's hit!" Herschel's voice was broken. She looked over her shoulder, biting her lip. Herschel knelt above William, who flailed and writhed, holding his arm.

The other children were crying as teachers tried to drag them back inside the safety of the school.

Numbly Laura clutched the sobbing Janine closer to her chest. She forced herself to look at the old gentleman again. He lay motionless on the sidewalk in the welter of his blood.

His beautiful overcoat is ruined, she thought illogically. And just as illogically, a line from *Macbeth* ran through her head: *"Who'd have thought the old man to have so much blood in him?"*

So much blood.

Then, with a shock, she realized that Trace and Rickie still hung onto the fence as if hypnotized, staring at the corpse. They alone of all the children were not crying or shrieking.

They regarded the dead man, the dark pool of blood, the screaming wounded woman, with wooden faces. Their hands still gripped the fence bars, and a slow, thin stream of scarlet ran down Trace's cheek, dropping to stain the bright blue of his coat.

Oh, God, he's shot, Laura thought in panic. She rose and stumbled to the boys although Janine screamed out for her to stay.

Quickly she examined Trace's cheek. It bled profusely, but he didn't seem to notice. He acted irritated that she had pulled him away from the fence.

Janine got to her feet and lurched toward Laura, hysterical. She grasped her around the waist and wouldn't let go. "Shh, shh," Laura told the girl, her voice shaking. "We'll go inside. We'll be fine inside."

Rickie, too, was annoyed to be pulled away from

the fence rails and clung to them more tightly. "Shots," he said. "Shots. The man got shooted on the hundred-and-twenty-ninth step."

"Yes, yes," she said impatiently, wrenching him from the fence. She was terrified that whoever had opened fire would return and shoot again.

She wrapped on arm around the bleeding Trace, the other around Rickie. Janine still hung onto her waist, wailing hysterically.

In the distance, sirens shrilled. "The police are coming," she told the children, struggling to herd them inside. "The police will be here, and we'll be safe."

"The car come by," Rickie said, frowning studiously. "The car shot. Hit the man."

Trace touched his own cheek, then regarded his bloodied glove impassively. He nodded. "The car shot. Hit the man."

A drive-by shooting. Here—in front of our own school, in front of these poor children, Laura thought. *The world's gone crazy. The world's mad.*

Somehow, Laura maneuvered her little brood inside the school.

"I've called nine-one-one," Mrs. Marcuse, the school's director, said, struggling to exert control. "The police will be here. An ambulance will be here." She held up her hands as if beseeching them for peace, but there was none.

Jilly, the oldest student, crouched in a corner, hugging herself, her expression full of terror. She covered her eyes with her hands, as if she could block out what she had witnessed.

Oh, my God, that they should see this—Laura

thought, still in shock—*that children should see such a thing*.

Laura knelt before Trace. She snatched off her muffler and dabbed it against his cheek. "Does it hurt?" she asked.

He ignored her question. He frowned at the door. "Car shot thirty times," he said, jutting his lower lip out petulantly. "Hit the man nineteen. The man didn't finish the walk. Got to finish the walk."

"He can't finish his walk. Trace, look at me. Tell me if you're hit any place else. Do you hurt anywhere else?"

Stolid, he didn't answer. He stared at the door instead, and Laura thought that maybe the wound in his cheek was only superficial. She kept her muffler pressed against it, willing her hand not to shake.

"I saw the license," Rickie said quietly. "It was MPZ one oh four eight one nine."

Trace nodded. "MPZ one oh four eight one nine. The man should finish the walk."

The hall was overwarm, almost stifling, but Laura suddenly went cold. Once more a peculiar silence enclosed her, blocking the riot of sound.

"What?" She clutched Trace's jacket by the lapel. "Say that to me again."

He frowned more irritably. "MPZ one oh four eight one nine. The man should finish the walk."

Her heart beat painfully hard as she turned to Rickie. "You saw the license number?"

"MPZ one oh four eight one nine," he said.

My God, she thought with a rush of adrenaline. *They both got the license number.*

SCOUNDREL

by Elizabeth Elliott
author of THE WARLORD

**In a world of war and intrigue,
the greatest danger of all is in
daring to love. . . .**

Lady Lily Walters played her part to perfection. Her low-cut gowns and empty chatter kept everyone from guessing the truth—that this sensuous flirt was really a spy. Willingly, she risked her life to pass on vital secrets only she could divulge. But when the dangerously attractive Duke of Remmington took her in his arms, she found herself wishing just once she could drop her masquerade and show him the woman that she really was. . . .

"Well, I'm in no hurry to find myself in a state that makes most men I know positively morose. Although I'll admit that—" Harry stopped in midsentence. "Good God. Will you look at that."

Remmington turned around at his friend's insistence. One could see almost anything on the streets of London, but his face registered surprise at the sight that greeted him.

The new gaslights of Saint James's Street revealed the shadowy form of a woman as she raced down the middle of the foggy street, her figure vague and muted in the dim light. He watched with an eerie sense of the surreal as she drew nearer and her features became distinct.

The fog that surrounded her began to drift away, a trick of the eye that made her look as if she emerged from the night itself. The voluminous folds of a dark blue robe billowed out from her waist like silk sails in a brisk wind. The skirt of a pristine white nightgown revealed itself beneath the robe, and her flight outlined long, lithe legs against the smooth fabric. Waist-length auburn hair floated over her shoulders in fiery waves. One slender hand held the skirt of her robe and nightgown above the path of her slippered feet while the other hand clutched her throat. The expression on her face was one of sheer terror. She glanced over her shoulder several times, as though certain the hounds of hell were on her heels.

The girl was less than fifteen feet away when Remmington swore under his breath, recognizing the shadowy figure at last. He thought she was running right to him, but she changed direction at the last moment, obviously intent on the entrance to White's. Two long strides from the side of the carriage and he intercepted her. He caught her with one outstretched arm and her breath came out in a whoosh. He pushed her toward Harry and the waiting carriage.

"Get her inside, man. She can't be seen on the street!" Remmington spun around to face the club's doorman. The liveried servant's mouth hung wide open. He pressed ten pounds into the man's palm. "One word of this incident and I will know where to direct my anger."

Remmington didn't think it possible, but the man's eyes actually opened wider as he stared at the money.

"No! My father!" the girl cried out. She tried to pull away from Harry's grip. Her voice sounded strained, and she put her hand again to the high, ruffled neckline of her nightgown. She turned her attention to Remmington, both hands at her neck now as if she found it painful to speak. "He's . . . inside."

"No, he isn't," Remmington replied.

Harry stared down at the woman in silence, his expression incredulous. "Good God! Lady—"

"Shut up," Remmington snapped. He turned Harry toward the door to his carriage. "Just get her inside before anyone else sees her."

Harry pushed Lady Lillian into the plush carriage and took the seat opposite hers. Remmington followed a moment later, then he signaled to the driver with a rap on the roof before he sat next to Lily. She clutched at his arm as the carriage lurched forward, but pushed away from him as soon as she regained her balance. Her breath came in quick pants and he could feel her tremble. The fear in her eyes made him uneasy.

"Would you mind telling us just what you are doing on the streets at this time of night?"

"Must find . . ." She lifted her hand to her throat. Her words died on a hoarse whisper. ". . . Papa."

He reached out to push aside the lacy frills that concealed her neck. She slapped his hand away, but not quickly enough. The ugly red marks on her throat made him swear under his breath. Someone had tried to strangle her! Rage flowed through him, instant and potent, but he forced his voice to remain calm. "Who did this to you, Lily?"

Harry leaned forward. He'd also noticed the bruises. "Give us the name and we'll take care of the blackguard."

"Don't . . . know. Must . . . find—"

"There, there, Lillian," Harry said. "We'll take you home to Crofford House and get to the bottom of this foul deed." Harry leaned forward to place his hand over hers, but Lily jerked away and pressed herself even further into the corner of the carriage.

"No!" She shook her head.

"We're not going to hurt you," Remmington murmured. "We only want to help you, Lily. Are you afraid that whoever did this is still in your house?"

Her gaze moved slowly to Harry, then back again before she finally nodded. Remmington covered her hand before he remembered that she'd refused the same meager comfort from Harry. He was absurdly pleased when she didn't draw away from him. "How many were there?"

"I saw . . . one," she said with difficulty. "I screamed . . . no one came. Please take—"

"How many servants are in residence?"

"Seven."

Remmington frowned. Not an unusually large number of servants, but enough that one should have heard her cries for help. Harry's comment echoed his thoughts.

"It seems unlikely that just one man could take care of seven servants."

Lily tugged on Remmington's sleeve. "Papa is at White's."

He winced at the sound of her raspy voice, then slowly shook his head. "No, Lily. I saw your father leave White's an hour ago. Where else might he be?"

Her expression grew uncertain. "I don't know."

He exchanged a worried glance with Harry, then nodded toward the trapdoor in the ceiling. "Tell the driver to take us to my house."

Harry stood up to carry out the order, but Lily shook her head. "I cannot—"

"We will stop just long enough to get some of my men," Remmington told her, "then we will all go check on your servants. If your father doesn't turn up in the meantime, I will send someone out to search for him."

She nodded, but her hands were clenched in tight fists, her lower lip caught between her teeth. There was a look of bewildered fear in her eyes. As he gazed down at her stricken face, he was nearly overwhelmed by the need to take her into his arms and keep her safe. He wanted to kill the man who did this to her.

"Can you describe the man who attacked you?" His frustration deepened when she shook her head. "Can you remember anything at all? The color of his eyes? His height or size? Are you certain it was not a servant, or someone you know?"

Her breaths became more rapid and shallow with each question. She held one hand to her throat, the other to her forehead.

"Take a deep breath," he ordered, worried she would faint. He knew from his experience in battles that anyone frightened this badly would respond more readily to command than to pity. "That's right. Now take one more and you'll feel better."

She took several before her breathing returned to a more normal rate. "Too many . . . questions. No answers."

He didn't quite believe her. She had to remember something. She must be too shaken to recall the answers clearly at the moment, but he didn't know how to calm her down.

"We need a plan. Give me a moment to think this through." Unable to concentrate when he looked at her, he pushed aside the carriage curtains and gazed out at the night. He closed his eyes and pictured the marks that lined her throat. By tomorrow, they would be dark, vicious bruises. He couldn't imagine that any sane man would take that slender throat between his hands to deliberately choke the life from her. He could think of any number of things a man might want to do to a beautiful, defenseless woman, but murder was not one of them.

His hands became fists as he wondered just what sort of man she'd encountered. Perhaps she'd stumbled across a common thief, startled him enough that he'd turned on her. Only a fool would rob a house when the family was in residence, yet who else would try to kill her? It was a daring plan, but a definite possibility. If a thief knew that Lily and her father were at a ball, it would be logical to assume they would remain there until the very early hours of the morning. Yet that night Lily had gone home early, and Remmington knew the reason why.

His gaze returned to her. If he hadn't interfered in her life earlier that evening, she might still be at the Ashlands' ball. Without thinking, he reached out to stroke her cheek. "Don't worry, Lily. You're safe now."

On sale in February:

GUILTY AS SIN
by Tami Hoag

BREATH OF MAGIC
by Teresa Medeiros

IVY SECRETS
by Jean Stone

To enter the sweepstakes outlined below, you must respond by the date specified and follow all entry instructions published elsewhere in this offer.

DREAM COME TRUE SWEEPSTAKES

Sweepstakes begins 9/1/94, ends 1/15/96. To qualify for the Early Bird Prize, entry must be received by the date specified elsewhere in this offer. Winners will be selected in random drawings on 2/29/96 by an independent judging organization whose decisions are final. Early Bird winner will be selected in a separate drawing from among all qualifying entries.

Odds of winning determined by total number of entries received. Distribution not to exceed 300 million.

Estimated maximum retail value of prizes: Grand (1) $25,000 (cash alternative $20,000); First (1) $2,000; Second (1) $750; Third (50) $75; Fourth (1,000) $50; Early Bird (1) $5,000. Total prize value: $86,500.

Automobile and travel trailer must be picked up at a local dealer; all other merchandise prizes will be shipped to winners. Awarding of any prize to a minor will require written permission of parent/guardian. If a trip prize is won by a minor, s/he must be accompanied by parent/legal guardian. Trip prizes subject to availability and must be completed within 12 months of date awarded. Blackout dates may apply. Early Bird trip is on a space available basis and does not include port charges, gratuities, optional shore excursions and onboard personal purchases. Prizes are not transferable or redeemable for cash except as specified. No substitution for prizes except as necessary due to unavailability. Travel trailer and/or automobile license and registration fees are winners' responsibility as are any other incidental expenses not specified herein.

Early Bird Prize may not be offered in some presentations of this sweepstakes. Grand through third prize winners will have the option of selecting any prize offered at level won. All prizes will be awarded. Drawing will be held at 204 Center Square Road, Bridgeport, NJ 08014. Winners need not be present. For winners list (available in June, 1996), send a self-addressed, stamped envelope by 1/15/96 to: Dream Come True Winners, P.O. Box 572, Gibbstown, NJ 08027.

THE FOLLOWING APPLIES TO THE SWEEPSTAKES ABOVE:

No purchase necessary. No photocopied or mechanically reproduced entries will be accepted. Not responsible for lost, late, misdirected, damaged, incomplete, illegible, or postage-die mail. Entries become the property of sponsors and will not be returned.

Winner(s) will be notified by mail. Winner(s) may be required to sign and return an affidavit of eligibility/release within 14 days of date on notification or an alternate may be selected. Except where prohibited by law, entry constitutes permission to use of winners' names, hometowns, and likenesses for publicity without additional compensation. Void where prohibited or restricted. All federal, state, provincial, and local laws and regulations apply.

All prize values are in U.S. currency. Presentation of prizes may vary; values at a given prize level will be approximately the same. All taxes are winners' responsibility.

Canadian residents, in order to win, must first correctly answer a time-limited skill testing question administered by mail. Any litigation regarding the conduct and awarding of a prize in this publicity contest by a resident of the province of Quebec may be submitted to the Regie des loteries et courses du Quebec.

Sweepstakes is open to legal residents of the U.S., Canada, and Europe (in those areas where made available) who have received this offer.

Sweepstakes in sponsored by Ventura Associates, 1211 Avenue of the Americas, New York, NY 10036 and presented by independent businesses. Employees of these, their advertising agencies and promotional companies involved in this promotion, and their immediate families, agents, successors, and assignees shall be ineligible to participate in the promotion and shall not be eligible for any prizes covered herein. SWP 3/95

DON'T MISS THESE FABULOUS
BANTAM WOMEN'S FICTION TITLES